Pennies on the Tracks

By
Danny Lee Ingram

PublishAmerica
Baltimore

First printing

ISBN: 1-4137-2286-5
PUBLISHED BY PUBLISHAMERICA, LLLP
www.publishamerica.com
Baltimore

Printed in the United States of America

To Tom and Edith, my parents.

Table of Contents

Reunion

Bill sat silent, watching the panorama of corn fields flow past the train window. No one sat beside him, but he didn't mind. It was his first ride in a long time, and he was enjoying every minute of it. He smiled slightly as a thousand golden tassels waved in the wind. Those tassels would soon be gone, but Bill thought of all the perennial friends he had known, loved for a while, then told good-bye, and he knew in his heart that they were still out there somewhere, thriving, reaching for the sun. It was a field full of faces and towns, laughter and tears.

The train rocked gently from side to side, the quiet roar of the steel wheels rolling along forgiving tracks, almost hypnotic, soothing. The intermittent wail of the train's horn several cars ahead brought back memories of that old trestle where he and Sammy used to play after school. They would lay pennies on the tracks and hide under the weathered beams till the train passed over. Then they would climb up and recover their flattened treasures. Bill had loved the trains, and he knew those tracks would someday be his escape route from Buford, a little town that was nothing more than a social center for a thousand prisoners of the corn.

He hadn't heard from Sammy since their graduation day at Buford High. The class was small, thirty-four if he remembered correctly, and hadn't changed much during its four years. Almost all of the classmates cried and hugged as though they would never see each other again, like a family saying their last good-byes. Bill had cried, too, but he knew he had to get away, far away down those tracks, that is if he was ever going to be anybody.

The train slowed and clanked past a lone pickup truck on an otherwise deserted street. Whatever town it was looked sort of like Buford, the way Bill remembered it anyway, five or six stores on each side of "Main Street," with last year's fashions and this year's prices. He had rented his cap and gown at a store like that. The gown had been way too big and the cap too small, but he hadn't cared. He had just wanted to get the whole business over with as quickly as possible.

He guessed that some of the class must have seen each other by now, but not him. Somehow, they had always tracked him down every ten years with letters about reunions. And he had always planned on returning. But after thinking about it long and hard, he would decide to wait till the next reunion, thinking that times would be better by then.

The train sped up again, and the little town was swallowed by the encroaching corn fields. Bill watched the last silo disappear from view as the train veered a little to the left on its short cut through the fields, away from the roads.

But times never got much better. Sure, he had worked at factories and farms, and even had a couple of businesses of his own, a record store and a flower shop, but things never seemed to work out the way he planned. Before he ever thought seriously about making a go of it, he had already sold out and climbed into whatever old car he had at the time and headed down the road toward some other dream.

He fell in love twice, even married once, but that didn't work out either. There was something about being tied to one spot or one person for a long time that always caught up with him, tugged and tugged away at his sleeve till he finally gave in and left everything behind.

The sun had sunk low and was bobbing on the distant waves of corn when that twinge rose in his chest again. Bill knew he shouldn't have eaten that hot dog at the station. The heartburn had been flaring up a lot lately, and he pulled out a half-roll of Tums from his shirt pocket and popped two into his mouth. They didn't help much. He grimaced as he chewed and swallowed the bland chalkiness and stuck the roll back into his pocket.

He turned toward the window and noticed his reflection staring back at him. Thirty years. He just couldn't believe it. His graying-brown hair had receded, and deep wrinkles lined his forehead, permanent wrinkles as though he were constantly considering some important decision. His eyes had lost their dreamer's sparkle long ago, now seeing almost nothing but memories through the dull blue. He wore a gray-checkered shirt, faded, but clean, as clean as his baggy, khaki work pants. He had washed them both by hand the day before and left them to dry on the porch rail of the migrant shack.

In his lap he held his only luggage, a wrinkled, brown paper bag with only two things inside—his high school yearbook and the thirty-year reunion invitation he had received a month earlier. The yearbook cover was ragged and the pages stained and torn, but the people in it were still as young as ever. But Bill knew they had changed. He wished they hadn't. He hadn't wanted to grow older either.

A woman and little boy hurried past Bill's seat, the boy squirming, tugging at his mother's sleeve with one hand and holding his crotch with the other. The woman glanced over at Bill as she passed, and smiled. Bill smiled back, but she was already gone. He thought of her kind, unwrinkled face and of those nights he had sat alone in the shack in the weak glow of a kerosene lamp, staring at the pictures of his old classmates. Would they even remember him? Would they be glad to see him? Or would they whisper across the room and pretend to talk about something else when he looked their way? They probably had their own families now. Nice cars and houses and big, important jobs. But Bill had finally decided that all of that was okay. He knew he still had chances of his own. He was just a little behind the others, but he still had dreams. And one of those dreams was going to pay off, someday.

He had emptied the small jar he kept hidden behind a loose board in the shack and bought a ticket all the way to New Orleans. New Orleans—he just knew things would change for the better there. And he knew it was a good omen that the train station had a whole stack of brochures about that town. He glanced down at the brochure lying on the seat beside him and smiled. Pictures of jazz bands and sunny streets and tourists in funny makeup, smiling and having a great time. Yes, something better was waiting for him there. He would stop over in Buford, go to the reunion with his New Orleans dream, and catch the next train out the following day.

The golden glow of the fields was fading quickly, the sun having disappeared over the horizon, and Bill realized that he was massaging his arm, numb and useless. He just figured that he was tired, and part of his body was already falling asleep. He knew that Buford couldn't be more than another half hour away, so he thought he would take a little nap before he saw all of his old friends again. Glancing out the window, he saw that night was coming on even quicker now, and he laid his head back on the seat and closed his eyes.

Soon, he had drifted off to sleep and found himself walking along a peaceful, country road beside some railroad tracks. He waved as a train sped by, unusually quiet, and there in one of the windows was Sammy, waving back and smiling and motioning for Bill to come along. Bill waved even more and gave Sammy an exaggerated nod and walked on and watched as the train disappeared down the distant tracks. But the heartburn came again. He didn't have any Tums, and he was tired, very tired. He walked to the side of the road and lay down in the tall grass beside the corn field. He just needed a little nap—that's all. A little nap before he got to Buford, or was it New Orleans? It didn't matter because with a little nap the heartburn would go away.

As the train slowed and approached the station, the conductor walked down the aisle announcing, "Next stop, Buford." He passed a quiet, slumbering man, sitting alone and holding a wrinkled brown bag. The conductor started to tap the man on the shoulder, but then he noticed a New Orleans brochure lying on the seat beside him. The man looked so peaceful that the conductor decided not to disturb him and walked away announcing Buford in a quieter tone.

Two passengers rushed by the slumbering man, a woman with a suitcase and a little boy, the boy tugging at her sleeve. Soon, the train jerked slightly, pulling out of the Buford station, and the man's wrinkled bag slipped and fell to the floor. But the man sat still, his eyes closed, his hands lying empty on his lap.

The train passed over a trestle on the edge of town, where little boys used to lay pennies on the tracks and dream of places far away. And the steel wheels rolled faster and faster, and the horn wailed deeper and deeper into the darkness of the corn. And the unseen tassels waved, as the train rushed away, leaving Buford behind for the lights of New Orleans.

Dogwood Fence

Jack sighed heavily as his old pickup coughed and sputtered, even after he had stopped and turned off the switch. He glanced down at his oversized, digital, three-dollar watch: 5:30 p.m.

He rubbed his back and stretched as he walked around to the truck bed. The boards had bounced half-out but still lay balanced on the tailgate. He pulled them out and stacked them in their usual spot beside the truck.

The phone rang inside his trailer, and Jack ambled in and picked up the receiver. His boss. Yes, he had taken down the alley fence. Yes, he'd paint the pieces before their next construction job tomorrow. Yes, he knew they had to keep the kids out. No, he had no idea who painted that stuff on there last night.

Jack looked back out at the boards. He shuffled the junk under the kitchen sink and pulled out a gallon of light brown paint and a brush still in plastic.

He sat down for a moment at the table, sighing again, loud in the empty trailer. Outside, birds sang and squirrels barked, but his sigh drowned out everything.

Leaning the wood against the skeletal remains of an old shed, he rebuilt the alley fence. Then he stood back and looked at it. He squinted at the evening light then rearranged the boards until the picture came to life again. It was an advertisement—MUST SELL FRESH LITTER OF MUTTS. CALL AFTER 6 P.M.

Jack unwrapped the brush and popped open the paint lid. The paint swirled putrid on the surface, so he picked up a fallen branch and stirred the brown slime. Finally, he dipped the brush into the paint and swiped it a couple of times on the can's edge.

The birds sang and the squirrels barked as Jack raised the brush, but then he stopped. MUTTS. FRESH LITTER. He looked around at the squirrels and at the birds, and they looked back at him, and he looked around at the wide-open woods that surrounded him. Then he looked back at the empty trailer, its open, empty door, and glanced down at the almost faded white line on his empty finger.

Jack put the lid back on the paint, laid the brush on top, and jogged to the trailer and into the bathroom. He took the extra roll of toilet paper from the shelf and dug his fingers into the cardboard tube, pulling out a small wad of bills. Two hundred twenty dollars. He counted it again, two hundred twenty dollars, and stuffed the wad into his pocket.

He grabbed a pen and ran back out to the fence and wrote down the phone number right on his hand. FRESH LITTER OF MUTTS. Jack hurried back into the trailer and glanced down at his oversized, digital, three-dollar watch: 6:01 p.m. Smiling, he laughed out loud, but it wasn't loud, and the trailer wasn't empty, and the sun beamed right through the open door, and Jack suddenly remembered how to whistle, just as he reached for the phone.

Winesaps

The devil is beating his wife. That's what we used to say when sunlight and rain poured down together like this. But even though it's raining, it's still eighty degrees. The front porch of this old shack with its rails lying around in rotten pieces feels like an open sauna, steam rising from decayed wood and the parched earth. Overhead, hot, wet sunbeams filter through holes where the Appalachian winds peel back the shingles a little more each year. I'm standing in the only dry spot left.

I had planned to fix up the place someday, ever since Grandpa left it to me, but save a little, spend a lot—on everything else, and the years slipped away as the old house wrinkled and cracked, and the sun and rain moved in. Besides, tearing down these boards myself would be ripping away too much, so I've just let it be. And now that the sale will be final in a few days, I thought I'd visit for one last time.

Grandpa built this house by hand with those tall Georgia pines that once stood just past the meadow. He must have told me the story a hundred times, but I didn't mind, how he chopped and trimmed and hauled them back here with an old brown mule named Sam. I'd sit on the rail, and Grandpa would pull a sweet gum twig from the chest pocket of his overalls and roll it a few times between his thumb and forefinger. Then he'd shake his head and laugh, leaning back in that old rocking chair while he bit into the sweet gum and remembered old Sam.

"He weren't stubborn," he'd say. "He went way past that. Down right ornery, he was."

Grandpa said when Sam got tired that old mule would just sit right down and wouldn't budge till he got good and ready.

"I'd yell at him, throw water on him, even pop him on his big fat be-hind with a switch. But all he'd do was swing his head around and try to bite me."

Grandpa said he'd just leave Sam and walk back and work on the house, and sooner or later that mule would finally stand up and drag the log on in, and Grandpa would slip him an apple or two.

One day Sam sat down and never got up again. There's a short wooden slab still standing out there that Grandpa cut and carved from that last log. Before it got so old and faded, I could still read it.

"Sam, d. 1909. Got tired but now he's resting."

There were a few times just before sundown that I saw Grandpa walking out past the meadow. I'd follow him at a distance, and when he'd head back toward the house, I'd retrace his steps. There'd always be a shiny fresh apple lying at the base of that wooden slab.

When Grandpa told the story about building the house, he'd always end with Sam sitting down for the last time, and I figured he wanted to be alone for a bit, so I'd think of something else to go do. But there was one evening, and only one evening, when things changed.

It was twenty-two years ago, and I was only fourteen. I was here for one of my summer visits and was sitting on the rail as usual when all of a sudden Grandpa stopped right in the middle of a sentence. He just sat there staring out toward the meadow, and when I looked, there was this big doe staring right back at the house. I turned to Grandpa and started to speak, but he held up one hand and with the other took the twig from his mouth and dropped it over the rail. Then I noticed that he was actually turning pale.

"Are you okay?" I asked.

"Sh-h-h!"

He rose slowly from his chair.

"Stay here."

He stepped down from the porch and walked quietly across the yard and into the meadow toward the doe. Of course, I couldn't just sit there. I was already sneaking along back behind him, keeping him between me and that deer, peeking around the line of his shoulder now and then and thinking I was actually hidden.

The doe didn't move as we approached, except for a slight nod at times, and Grandpa walked slower the closer he got. He must not have known I was behind him because he never looked back. He just kept on walking. Then he slowly spread his arms out by his sides, his palms open toward the doe. Then he stopped and stood about fifty feet from the deer. I stopped behind him. His voice quivered and sounded even older than *he* was, as he began to speak.

"I didn't know."

The deer stared straight at him, never moving.

"Please forgive me. I told you before. I truly didn't know."

By that time I was leaning and gawking at this sight, and the deer's gaze left Grandpa and settled on me. I lost my balance and stumbled, and Grandpa turned and saw me. He motioned for me to stay put. But the deer didn't run. It stared at me with a look I will never forget.

"My grandson," said Grandpa, but the doe's gaze did not leave me.

A thousand thoughts raced through my mind as we three stood there at the far edge of the meadow, just a few yards from Sam's resting place, but none of the thoughts made any sense. And there was something about that deer's eyes. Something unusually light in the deep shadows of those foothills. Grandpa quietly cleared his throat and spoke to the deer again.

"I'll tell him. I'll tell him so he can carry it on and not forget."

The deer looked back and forth between us a couple of times then over at Sam's spot and at the shiny red Winesap Grandpa had left that day.

"Go ahead. He won't mind," Grandpa said, nodding toward the apple and toward Sam.

But the deer just looked back at us for a couple of seconds, snorted mist into the cool mountain air, and suddenly bounded off into the woods, its lope quickly fading till there was nothing but the distant screams of blue jays somewhere in the treetops. Grandpa was already walking past my shoulder before I even realized he had turned to leave, and not knowing what to say, I followed dumbly behind him.

When we got back to the porch, Grandpa sat back down in the chair without looking up at me and pulled another sweet gum twig from his pocket. He just stared at the twig for a minute, rolling it back and forth

15

between his fingers, then raised it and started chewing lightly on the green tip.

"Wha—" was all that I got out before he raised his hand again and motioned me back onto the rail. He stared out at the spot where we'd just been and nodded.

"That's Emma," he said. "I guess she figures it's time I told you."

"Told me what?" I asked, but he had such a far away look in his eyes I decided to just listen. The first whippoorwills and tree frogs and crickets were chiming in across the meadow when he began his story.

Did I ever tell you about my old friend Farley Gaines? We grew up together down by Big Creek. Yep, he's buried in the same row with your grandma. I'll show you his spot next time we go up there.

Anyway, Farley and me used to hunt these woods all around here. We was the same age, and the Gaines land run up against ours about a mile through them woods yonder. Our pa's bought us rifles the same year, and we learned how to shoot together. Squirrels, rabbits, coons, yep, you name it—we'd hunt it. I had a Blue Tick named Scratch, 'cause he was always itchin', and Farley had a mutt named Fuzz. Ugliest, hairiest dog I ever seen, but he had a good nose. Put the four of us together, and we couldn't be beat.

Up the road about another mile was the Hartleys. It was just an old man and his wife, and I couldn't understand why Papa told me to stay away from there. He said he'd heard stuff about 'em, but he'd never say what.

"Just stuff," he'd say and walk away. I seen them in town, though. They looked okay to me. I even walked up to the old lady's buckboard one day while her husband was fetchin' supplies in the General.

"Howdy," I said. "I'm Andy Jackson."

She jerked her head around, but then she smiled, dusted off her flour sack dress, and said, "Good morning, Andrew. I'm Mrs. Hartley."

I didn't notice much else about her but her eyes. She had the deepest, pale blue eyes I ever seen, and I couldn't help but stare. I can't even remember the rest of her face to this day. About that time her husband walked out with a big sack of sunflower seeds and a salt block and loaded 'em onto the wagon.

Mrs. Hartley looked back at her husband and said, "Jim, this is Andrew."

The old man looked me up and down for no more than a second and frowned and said, "Yeah, well you best be gettin' home. Your pa's probably got chores a-waitin'." And he climbed up on the wagon, clicked, and they pulled off down the street.

I just stood there like an idiot in the middle of the street for a minute 'cause I seen somethin' that I just couldn't figure out. That old man had the exact same kind of eyes that his wife had. I finally got out of the street when another wagon driver started cussin' me, and I decided that, well, that's probably how they got matched up. They liked each others eyes.

That was really the only time I saw them in person. They kept to themselves back in them woods, didn't bother nobody, and nobody bothered them. And I didn't think much about those eyes for a long time, except for that evenin' at the supper table I did tell Papa. Papa got all quiet-like at first and laid down his fork, and Mama just sat there starin' at me.

"What's wrong?" I asked. "They seem nice enough to me, except maybe for Mr. Hartley. He seems a bit prickly. Farley said—"

"I don't care what Farley said."

Papa's handlebar mustache was twitchin', and his mustache always twitched when he was real serious or mad. But when he was mad, he yelled. But he wasn't yellin'. He just twitched.

"You stay away from them people and stay off their land. I catch you on their land I'll take that gun away from you for keeps. And you won't be runnin' around with that Farley Gaines no more either."

I opened my mouth but closed it quick. I figured the best thing for me to do with all that twitchin' was not to ask any questions. I looked over at Mama, and she had her eyes closed and was sayin' somethin' that I couldn't make out.

Well, I figured that there was plenty other places to hunt, so I just looked back down at my plate and dug into that rabbit that me and Farley shot. There weren't any sense in causin' a big argument at the table anyway. But the real reason was that I didn't want Papa to start twitchin' and yellin' 'cause that might lead to the strap.

The next day I told Farley about it, and he said his pa was the same way. Said his pa told him not to ever look straight into them Hartley eyes. Somethin' about bad luck. Course, I had to just laugh it off 'cause I already looked both of them straight in the eyes. I mean it wasn't like I broke a mirror or walked under a ladder. Besides, me and Farley both had blue eyes, and so did half of our families. Not pale blue like them Hartleys, but blue just the same. So what was the big deal?

After that, Farley and me would joke with each other all the time sayin', "You look at me—I'll give you the hex!"

Well, things went on pretty normal after that till the day before Thanksgivin'. Me and Farley was out huntin' wild turkeys 'cause we was tryin' to make a little money for Christmas comin' up. Turkeys ain't hard to shoot if they're standin' still, but you spook 'em, and they'll flap and fly up a little and back down so quick it's hard to get a bead on 'em.

We coulda borrowed shotguns from our pa's, but then we couldn't brag about being marksmen. And we coulda tied up Scratch and Fuzz, but then we just didn't feel like the whole team. Besides, we were too far back in them woods to go lookin' for rope.

So, we'd find a flock, and before we could get a bead, Scratch and Fuzz would be chasin' turkeys everywhere, feathers flyin', barks and gobbles, gobbles and barks, and we couldn't even shoot 'cause we was afraid we'd hit the dogs. But it was a funny sight, and we'd be laughin' so hard and gobblin' we couldn't a-hit anything on purpose anyway.

After awhile, Farley said he thought we might be gettin' too close to Hartley land, but I said I thought it was farther on up the valley quite a ways, so we decided to go on deeper into the woods.

The sun had already been down for a little while, but it was still pretty light, when we heard some more turkeys through a thicket up ahead. We started pushin' on through when I heard a bark back behind me. Me and Farley turned around, and Scratch and Fuzz were just sittin' back there starin' at us.

I whispered, "Come on, Scratch," and patted my leg, but he just sat there and started whinin'. Farley called Fuzz, but Fuzz wouldn't come either.

"What's the matter with 'em?" I asked Farley, but he just shrugged, and the turkeys up ahead gobbled on. We decided to go on without the dogs, thinkin' that they must not want to go through that thicket and get cockleburs all over them.

When we came out on the other side, that's when we heard heavy footsteps. Me and Farley backed into the thicket and crouched down, and then I saw what every hunter dreams about. The biggest buck I ever seen or ever even heard of was walkin' through them woods toward the turkeys. It was at least a sixteen pointer, and I couldn't even imagine how much it weighed. It stopped a little ways off and just stood there watchin' them gobblers, but they didn't pay him no mind at all.

I started to raise my rifle, but Farley waved and got my attention. He pointed at my gun and made signs that my rifle was too small. I thought about it and knew he was probably right. That deer was so huge! But I just couldn't resist. I knew that there was one way to kill it, but I'd have only one shot. Farley shook his head no, but I nodded yes and put a finger to my lips.

I raised my rifle and aimed it straight at the buck's head. I gobbled real soft, but with all that commotion the turkeys were makin', he didn't hear me. So I gobbled louder. The buck turned his head around toward me, and from then on everything seemed like it was in slow motion.

I drew a bead right between his eyes. His eyes. They were huge and pale blue, and before I could stop myself, I squeezed the trigger. I jerked from the shot, and the buck's head reared back. Then his big antlers fell forward, real slow, and them blue eyes looked at me. He kept lookin' at me while his front legs buckled under him, and he keeled over and landed with a real loud thump—like thunder.

I looked at Farley, and Farley looked at me. He was sickly white, and I was shakin' all over. Then we heard it. Somethin' big runnin' through the trees towards the buck, towards us. Me and Farley jumped up at the same time and crashed through that thicket as hard as we could run.

Before we even reached the dogs, there was a real loud scream that sounded like a woman or some kinda animal, and it echoed all through them mountains. And whatever it was kept on screamin', but we kept on runnin', and then the dogs were runnin' with us. We didn't even slow down till we stopped at the front porch, and we was throwin' up and cryin' and hurtin' like crazy from runnin' so far. But what hurt worse was that we had to keep quiet. We knew we couldn't let anybody know, especially our pa's.

As far as I know, Farley never did say anything. And we didn't even talk about it to each other. And nobody ever heard from the Hartleys again. When they didn't show up for supplies for about a month, somebody went out to check on 'em and then went back and brought the sheriff. The story is that everything was just as it was supposed to be. Plates set for dinner, darnin' laid out over a chair, but whatever was cookin' was all dried up, and there hadn't been a fire in the fireplace for a long time.

Grandpa had been chewing on that sweet gum the whole time, and he took its frazzled remains out of his mouth and flipped them over the rail.

"There's a lot of strange things in this world," he said. "Things you won't understand and things you weren't meant to understand. You just got to deal with 'em whenever they come."

With that he got up and walked to the door.

But before he went in, he turned and said, "Someday this place is gonna be yours, and if Emma Hartley ever shows up, you'll know how to deal with her. She's a forgivin' woman, but she's gettin' old, and sometimes she forgets."

I didn't know what to say. Grandpa went on into the house, and I sat there alone till bedtime, staring into the shadows out past the meadow.

That's how I remember this old porch, Grandpa sitting out here telling me that story, the only story he ever told just once, looking out there toward Sam's resting place and where we stood while Grandpa talked to the deer.

I really hate to lose this place, but it seems I've had a streak of bad luck all my life. When this rain lets up a little more, I'm going to say good-bye for the last time, but before I leave, I've got a shiny red Winesap I'm going to leave for Sam. But if I were to come back in the morning, I know this apple would be gone. It always is.

Spee-lunking

Dangling at the end of a forty-foot rope, maybe a mile inside Willard's Cave, wasn't a usual part of our adventures, and every time I moved my arm or leg or anything, I started rotating, first one way then the other, like a telephone cord untwisting. With each turn, my stomach began to crawl up the rope, dragging Baker's chocolate right along with it. The chocolate was emergency food, in case of a cave-in, but my stomach had already caved-in from hunger, and I had been munching.

The rope ran around my back and under my arms and was tied in a fat, double-knot, just in case. I pulled myself up to relieve the pressure and started twisting again. Soon, I wondered if it was really me rotating or the cave walls revolving around me. My friend Joey was up top, yelling, "Stop moving around!" But he was too late, as usual.

Willard's Cave had become our private exploration, an escape from the high school humdrum, and for the past few weekends, we had squeezed down through the winding, wormhole entrance into the first cavern, as big as a tennis court. Every week we braved farther into the unknown, trekking deeper and deeper into the cave, marking our trail like Arne Saknussemm on our own journey to the center of the earth. But we never used the same marks, in case anyone got wise to our trail and tried to do us in. Sometimes we used a coded scratch of letters on the wall, sometimes an inconspicuous pile of stones, and sometimes, even a hidden candy wrapper. Larry, my other friend and cave exploring partner, was the best observer of all three of us, so it was up to him to add the notes of twists and turns and secret markers to the crude drawing he carried in a Zip-Loc bag for keeping our map dry.

It didn't take but a couple of trips in for us to learn to leave our jackets—hidden, of course—back near the entrance, since the cave was about fifty-two degrees all the time, and with all that crawling and climbing, we always worked up a sweat even without our jackets. But with nothing between me and that rope but long-johns under a flannel shirt, the rope dug deeper and deeper into my armpits, scratching and itching at the same time. They were separate little tortures, and I had to move around to put the itch under the scratch and vice versa, even if it meant plunging into the crevice below. The crash couldn't have been any worse.

"Stop moving around!" yelled Joey again.

Yeah, right. He always had the right advice—after the fact. He was one of those I-told-you-so's, but he never told-you-so. He just liked to rub things in. But he was okay, I guess. One of my best friends, along with Larry. Larry hadn't said much about the flashlight ordeal and had headed alone back through the cave to get some more rope from the car. After his head disappeared from the ledge above, I heard a couple of OOMPHs as he must have hurried too fast and slipped on the cave's muddy floor.

I looked down past my own muddy sneakers and straight into the light. Of all the ways a flashlight could land. It must have stuck in the mud with its six D-cells straight down, and the light was shining up at me as if I were caught in the act, which I was. It was humiliating enough to find out too late that the rope was too short, but there I was, the guilty, the accused, caught red-handed, or maybe dirty-handed, in the unforgiving beam of a cop's flashlight.

Joey's cop uncle had loaned it to him for some weird science project, but me and my big mouth had convinced Joey to bring it on our spee-lunking jaunt that day. Spee-lunking. I wasn't sure if that was a real word or not, but that's what we called it. I figured that whatever it was, it turned out me-lunking over the edge of that gorge to rescue the uncle's precious flashlight. But after all, it was me who had dropped it.

I had squirmed belly-down to the edge of the ledge and was poking the beam into the crevices below when the flashlight slipped from my grip and plunged into the darkness. Crash, then another crash, then a dull, echoing thump. That must have been when it stuck in the mud. I turned around, and Larry's light was shining on Joey. But only half of

Joey's head was lit—one bulging eye and half a gaping mouth, big enough for a barrel of bats. Joey said his uncle was going to kill him. I told him cops don't do that and not to worry. I'd go get it. Besides, it seemed like a big adventure to get lowered down into a part of the cave where no human had ever been. Sort of like the first man on the moon. But I didn't say that to Joey or Larry. I was afraid they might volunteer.

So there I was, floating slow-motion in space, waiting forever for Larry to get back with the rope. But hadn't it taken us two hours to get where we were? Yes, but that was with a lot of stopping and sidetracking and "scientific" observation of cave creatures and features. Sickly-white eyeless bugs, irate bats, stalactites and -mites—we still argued up and down over which was which, and moths, moths as big as my hand that would cling motionless to the cave walls and flop out in your face and scare the living crap out of you. And there were diamonds. We wished they were anyway. Millions of them, sparkling in clusters like chandeliers in some caverns, and sometimes running along the ceiling and down the wall. We wished we'd found the mother lode. But we hadn't. Not yet, anyway. But maybe....

The rope bit into my arm, and I flinched and ouched, and Joey stuck his beam right into my eyes.

"Move your light!" and "Stop moving around!" flashed back and forth till he moved it, and I could see again. I looked up and saw that same half of Joey's head, but he was too far away to see his eye. He got quiet again, and I noticed that all around it was very quiet. I was glad because the bats must have been sleeping, but then I thought that they could be quietly snickering in the dark at the fool on the rope who couldn't fly. I started twisting again and snapped out of my bat trance.

It was ridiculous. I couldn't just hang there all day. I looked around at the walls, and the light from below caused black shadows behind every protruding rock. I couldn't tell what half of the walls really looked like, so I told Joey to shine his light around. After blinding me again, he swung the beam so fast that my brain didn't register what I saw.

"Slow down!"

He did, and this time I could see and remember. Not far away was a craggy ledge that ran from about halfway down the wall practically to the floor. I told Joey there was no sense in waiting for Larry and that I was going to swing over to the wall and climb down. But he didn't say anything, just in case I fell or got stuck or something so he could rub it in later.

Sticking my legs out and pulling them back several times, before long I was a human pendulum in a subterranean pit. I swung back and forth, wider and wider, till my toes touched the wall, and I pushed back hard. On the next swing in, the back of my sneaker caught on the ledge, and for a minute, I just hung there, suspended from rope and rock. Lodging my other shoe as well, I slowly bent my legs, pulling myself toward the wall, till the ledge was within reach. I grabbed it and hoisted myself up sideways.

Soon I had the knot untied and let the rope swing back into the spotlight.

"Keep your light on me."

Joey did, and climbing down the ledge was no big deal. We had all climbed down a lot worse. I jumped the last three feet to the floor and sank up to my ankles in mud. I stood there stuck, breathing in the almost nauseating, damp air that I knew nobody had ever breathed before. I felt like a real explorer, first into the unknown.

My sneaker didn't budge when I raised my leg, and I tried to balance on one foot for about a second. I wavered and stepped down into the mud, sock and all. The hole where my shoe had lodged was already half filled with water, so I reached in, grabbed and pulled, but the mud was reluctant to give up its prey. My other shoe eased out of the mud without coming off, so with one shoe in hand, I squished over to the flashlight, still waiting there, beaming stupidly up at the empty rope. Yanking the light out of the mud, I wiped off the handle and decided I might as well look around since I was down there anyway. Pouring the water from the rescued shoe, I slipped it on, and the muddy cold made me shiver. That was okay. I was in real uncharted territory, and nothing could stop me now.

I eased farther down the crevice, away from Joey's beam, glancing back and forth from wall to wall as the passage narrowed. There wasn't much to see. No bugs, no bats, no moths, and especially no diamonds. As I rounded one corner, the passage opened up into another court-sized cavern with tunnels exiting in several directions. I passed the beam around the walls then suddenly woke from my precious explorer's dream. There next to one wall sat a small styrofoam cooler, its lid lying broken, beer cans partly submerged in the mud around it.

"Larry's got the rope!" echoed throughout the cave.

We tried to be careful about not making too much noise, cave-ins and all, but sometimes we forgot. But it didn't matter anyway. My discovery was a dud. I didn't care if the walls fell in. But then I thought, *They wouldn't know unless I told them. I mean I don't have to lie or anything. Being a little vague wouldn't be lying.*

"Let's go. I've got to get home." Joey had changed back to yelling in whispers.

I let him wait. He was just mad that he hadn't been the one to explore the new territory, especially since I had really made it. I poked the beam into a couple of the tunnels just for curiosity's sake, but mostly to keep Joey waiting a little longer. Finally satisfied that he must have been squirming, I headed back toward the crevice.

I glanced over my shoulder at the cavern one last time and thought of ways to justify my story later in case that someone else went down there. Someone could have left that cooler and the cans after I dropped the flashlight. Or there could have been a flood that washed everything down into that cavern from the upper rooms of the cave. Of course, it made sense to me.

"Not much to see down here anyway," I yelled back in a loud whisper. After all, I didn't want them spoiling my story. It was going to be my discovery, my footprints alone on my very own moon. I smiled toward the darkness to show the bats that I was no fool. Then I pointed the beam ahead and squished my way along the narrow passage back toward the rope, a cold-footed, mud-caked, spee-lunking master.

Choices

Michael sat silent, staring into the cracked mirror on the opposite wall of the barber shop, while Joe cleaned the electric clippers with an old, tattered toothbrush. Michael had heard it all before—the idle conversations of weather and women and politics. But he wasn't in the mood for talk, not today anyway.

"Sure looks like a gully-washer's coming," said Mr. Winters in the next chair.

"Yeah, it does," said Michael, smiling politely at Mr. Winters's reflection.

His gaze fell back upon his own image, split in two by the irregular crack. He didn't know exactly why he kept coming back to this little shop, whether it was for inspiration or reflection, but this is where his father had always brought him. The stench of witch hazel and cheap hair oil was still the same, and that worn-out chair was where he sat when his father, standing across the room by the coal heater, politicized the state of the world from his crackling, brimstone podium.

They all knew Michael, and they all laughed as usual when Joe asked, "Sure you want just a half inch off this time?"

"I'm sure," he answered as he had a hundred times, and eventually the snickers died down as they always did.

His hair was not long. It was already shorter than anyone's in the shop. He kept it that way because he liked feeling the wind against his scalp. It was stimulation to the brain for him. And he liked feeling those first drops of rain and the warm sunshine of a cool autumn day.

But they remembered. And so did he that his father convinced him that his sergeant would respect him more if he made a good first impression.

He had walked into the shop that morning, alone. He had been up all night, arguing with himself in the mirror, bunching his waist-length hair into pony tails and bouffants and even into sloppy pigtails. He didn't know how to braid. But when he left the barber shop, with his bloodshot eyes and beat-up suitcase, he knew that his father had been right.

"Don't do it," Bennie pleaded. "My cousin's got room for both of us in his van. He made that fake floor, and he won't charge us anything. We can be in Windsor tomorrow morning."

Michael didn't know what happened to Bennie's cousin, but Bennie sent letters from Leavenworth for the first couple of years. Michael never opened them and never wrote back.

He had walked into the shop that morning and sat in the chair where he had listened to his father's speeches. He felt the eyes of everyone on him as he stared at that long-haired reflection. Then he said to Joe, "Give me a GI."

The words echoed throughout his mind and throughout the shop and seeped through the floor and rushed downstream with the little creek that flowed underneath. Joe didn't say a word but nodded at Michael's reflection. The silence soon ended, and the others pretended to read their newspapers and hunting and fishing magazines, and some of them faked idle conversations about weather and women and politics.

Joe fumbled nervously with the scissors on the counter, knocking a comb onto the floor. He picked up the comb and dropped it into the Barbasol jar where it bobbed up and down in the putrid, green liquid. He took a long, deep breath and began carefully cutting Michael's hair in a straight line with the scissors. Michael winced as he watched the reflection of his long brown waves fall in slow motion to the shop floor and lie dead among the other fallen dead.

Then the clippers were hot on his neck, hot as the napalm that sheared the jungle where he lay half buried in the mud and rotting death. And they bit his neck, mosquitoes hungry for foreign cuisine, swarming about him, dive-bombing any spot of his skin not caked with mud.

He did his part. And he sneaked the disinfectant bleach from the supply shack and soaked the ragged pieces of tents till they were sickly white. And when he ran out of colors, he painted with the lives of his enemy, collected in a spare canteen till that night on patrol when he accidentally turned it up, and swallowed. He wretched and gagged and spit till his stomach writhed against its empty walls, and he fell to his knees as the canteen rolled into the darkness. But now his crimson and white masterpieces hung in bamboo frames in the houses of the rich, the distant. If they only knew. He knew. He knew he had gone too far—too far away, too far.

Michael stared into his cracked image once more as he got up from the chair.

"Whatcha paintin' today?" asked Joe as Michael handed him the usual three dollars.

"Well, Mr. Winters is usually right about the weather."

Mr. Winters smiled through a face full of lather.

"So, I'll probably just stay in and work on something from memory."

Michael walked past Bob Murphy combing the hair of his retarded son and stepped through the door into the breeze of the upcoming storm. He headed down the path by the stream as a shortcut home. The cool, moist air tingled his scalp as his mind wandered ahead through the ragged green canopy of darkening pines. He felt good knowing he had plenty of clean, white canvas and fresh, bright colors at home—blues and greens and yellows and purples. He'd find a memory, a good memory filled with all of those splendid, splendid colors, colors he had almost lost forever. And he felt even better, knowing that if all the reds were gone, he wouldn't mind at all.

Joe, the barber, was one of those pillars of the community who is, by his own choice, forever stuck at one end, and at the other, supports the impossible weight of the idea of citizen norm. But still, he was a likable sort. Although no one had ever known him to even take a vacation, he had always told stories of his trips to distant lands and of ocean voyages, and his war stories always aroused one's patriotic nature. After listening to one of his tales, one always left his shop with the epiphany and satisfaction of receiving the perfect haircut.

Underneath Joe's meticulously combed hair, sat the face of a drugstore cowboy—too smooth to have battled winter winds on the range, and yet, too large and too full of life to have done anything else. But he was not a cowboy. He was a barber—one of those pillars that holds up an obscure corner of the community building, essential but relatively unnoticed.

Joe's cowboy face never seemed quite right resting above his loud bow ties of bright greens and reds and blues. The white shirts he always wore made him appear like those typical southern politicians, always smiling at the ladies and kissing the fat cheeks of screaming babies. But underneath those smiles lay Joe's own private battle.

He had indeed left home when he was young. He had sailed the distant oceans and fought in foreign wars, but something had compelled him to come home—home to where his father had built the tiny barber shop on the remains of an abandoned, one-lane bridge. His father had cut hair for years, even throughout the Depression because barbering was one of those professions not affected much by Wall Street blunders. Just like the boom in the entertainment industry when people went out at night to forget their troubles, they would also get their hair cut to keep up appearances that everything was going okay. No one has ever heard of a rich barber, and if you don't have it to lose, you can't lose it.

As a child, Joe had sat on that wooden chair in the corner for hours, watching his father buzzing away with the electric clippers and talking about all of those important-sounding issues. Like so many youngsters that watched in awe as Joe cut their fathers' hair, Joe had wanted to be just like that—an important person in town that people talked to and listened to. But by the time Joe realized that barbering was a profession for unsung heroes, his compulsion had already dragged him home forever.

So there he dwelled, day after day, in that tiny shop over the stream. It was the center of male gossip and politics, and Joe was sometimes the all-important mediator of friendly disagreements and political debate, but his heart was secretly somewhere on the distant horizon. He wished sometimes that those ancient pillars that held up the shop would break away, and his little ark would rush him downstream and back to the sea. Passing by on a stormy day, one could sometimes see him staring longingly out the side window, watching the ripples in the rising stream hurdle over submerged rocks, racing away from his boring existence, and drop by drop, the very essence of his own being raced with them.

As Michael walked out through the barber shop door, Mr. Winters's smile slowly faded. He watched the dark clouds approaching over the Appalachian foothills, and he remembered watching those same skies on the morning of his twelfth birthday—a morning he would never forget.

"We're not going to be able to go fishing after church," his father chuckled. "Looks like it's gonna come down in pails."

But he had promised. Jimmy frowned. His father hated him. He knew it, and no matter what his mother said, he still knew it. It was his birthday, and his father insisted on ruining it for him. When would he ever get to use his new rod and reel?

Never, he thought.

"Now don't worry," his mother smiled. "It might clear up after all."

"Don't count on it," his father replied, thumbing through the TV guide.

Jimmy's mother just smiled and shook her head in mild disagreement.

"You'd better hurry and get ready," she said. "Those fish won't be biting if you miss church, and you know they're already in their own Sunday school."

Jimmy wanted to keep frowning, but he couldn't help but chuckle a little. His mother was always cracking little jokes like that. It seemed she could make him laugh, no matter what the situation. He loved his mother. But his father….

Baseball. Jimmy hated baseball, and he hated his father. Bill Winters had been a semi-pro player, and all he ever thought about was baseball. *He doesn't care one bit about his only child*, Jimmy thought. *He's always trying to make me into a little Bill*. But Jimmy couldn't catch. He couldn't throw, and he was too afraid of the pitches his father threw to even try batting.

"Why do you want to be such a fraidy-cat?" Bill asked him over and over again. "That little ball ain't gonna hurt you."

But Jimmy knew it could. He had seen the missing teeth and bleeding elbows of his schoolmates, brought on by this innocent child's game using that little ball. He wanted no part of it. He wished his father had gotten missing teeth and broken limbs when he had played. Then maybe he would understand better. Instead, his father hated him for not being a little Bill, and every chance he got, Bill made life miserable for him. At least, that's how Jimmy saw it.

Maybe someday, he would go to bat and use his father's head for a ball. That would show him. A home run right over the backyard fence. Yeah! Then he could go fishing and use his new rod and reel any time he wanted.

"We can't change the weather," his father said.

That's it, Jimmy thought. *He's lying.* He knew his father could change the weather, somehow, every time there was a big game on TV. So there Jimmy sat all afternoon staring at those teasing clouds that at times opened up and let the sun in for a wink of a moment. It never rained one drop, and his whole birthday was ruined.

That's when he decided to learn how his father did it. He wanted to ruin his father's day whenever there was a game in town. He starting reading about weather and climate and even majored in meteorology at college. But when his father died, and at the graveside his mother huddled him under her umbrella in the worst downpour in years, Jimmy felt so guilty that he dropped out of school and went to work in the cotton mill where he still works to this day.

As Michael disappeared from view, Henry Thomas smirked and shuffled in his chair, rattling his Wall Street Journal. He was the local banker and the only one with a shiny new Cadillac in the parking lot.

Typical lowlife, thought Henry. *He was a bum when we were in school, and he's still a bum. The army didn't do him any good, living up there in that shack, claiming to be shell-shocked or something and pretending to be some kind of goddamned artist. My kid sticks better stuff on the refrigerator. Why the hell doesn't he get a good job and fool around with paint on the weekends? No son of mine's gonna grow up like that. Probably living on food stamps and my goddamned taxes. People like him ought to be horsewhipped into working and stop being a burden on society.*

"Next," said Joe, brushing the clippings off Mr. Winters.

"How much for a trim?" asked Henry.

"Same as always," said Joe. "Three dollars."

i smell rain i want go home i want watch frogs daddy make me

"Charlie ready for a trim today?"

"Yep, he needs one. He's startin' to look like a girl."

i got hair my lip like tv no cut hair my lip

"I gotta take him to Milledgeville for a checkup Monday."

"You mean they're still afraid he might get outta hand?"

"They just don't know my Charlie like I do."

daddy smile i smile i want tree house tree backyard i want sit tree watch frogs sour green jar home no legs taste good not frogs no legs

"One of them new doctors thinks Charlie's just disturbed. I told him he's always been that way, but you know doctors."

chair cold i stick shorts not know where my pants big jar sour green

"You don't think they'll try to take him away from you, do you?"

"I won't let 'em. I've handled him all right for twenty-two years, and besides, something like that would just kill his mother."

"S'pose so."

not afraid buzz not bug bite me porch hears same i look

"Now, Charlie. You'll have to sit still."

all laugh bug bite man not bug shiny cut my hair oww hot

"Guess I'll have to use the scissors on him."

good buzz gone no hot shiny no buzz

"That's better. He just don't like those clippers. Kinda funny, don't you think? He wouldn't mind if I was to crop him bald. He just hates those clippers."

all laugh i laugh

"See what I told you, Joe? I think he understands a lot more than they give him credit for."

i broke my face mommy yell

"Uh, oh. There he goes again. I don't know what it is about this chair. He never cries in that other one, but sometimes he lets loose in this one. Here, let's move him over there."

mommy yell i cry

"Here you go, Charlie. Sit right down here."

not want broke face my face not broke man fixed my face i like man

"See, I told ya. Works every time. Don't know what it is about that chair."

i see rain window i want go home watch frogs frogs no hair frogs home i like frogs

Why the hell don't they just leave me alone? That damn Henry is such a snob now. He probably thinks I'm living on food stamps. Well, I've got news for him—I am. But I've got a secret. Just between me and this stream and these trees, I've got a little money stashed away for a rainy day, but I'm not going to tell the government about it. It's none of their business. I made it while I was doing their dirty work in Nam. And every time I sell a painting now, I make sure it's paid for in cold, hard cash. I don't take checks.

Henry must think I'm real stupid if he thinks I don't know what he says about me behind my back. Go ahead. Read your Wall Street. Strut around in your new Cadillac. I could buy one, too, if I wanted to. Cash. But I don't want to. I want to paint, and I want everybody just to leave me alone.

"When you graduate, you can get yourself a good job in the mill," Daddy said.

I looked at the gray around his temples and stared speechless into his tired, blue eyes. They had lost their sparkle long ago. I wondered why he wanted me to even think about it. Forty years is what he spent in that mill, and I was terrified at the thought of doing the same. I wondered sometimes if I really was lazy, or if I truly had a different calling.

Irresponsible? That's what my sister always called me. But how can you be irresponsible when you don't accept responsibility? She was only interested in the money aspect of everything. When I refused to tell her what my paintings brought, she just smirked and walked away, smug in thinking that I was making peanuts. Her new car. Her new clothes. Her blossoming bank account. So what? I could never make her understand that there are more important things—like doing what you really want to do.

"As long as you're living under my roof, you're going to cut that hair."

33

All he wanted was for me to look just like all those other blue collar lemmings racing off to the mill every day to dive off a cliff for those small town, small minded, management gods. If there ever was a caste system, it was in that little factory. Management had their side of town, and we in servitude, our side. And depending upon which side you were born to, you stayed for life. Most people accepted that as all there was. I didn't.

"Send your daddy's super an invitation," Mama said. "He'll get you something real nice."

I had seen the supervisor riding around town in his Mercedes, sticking his nose up at everyone. He didn't even know who I was. Why should he get me a graduation gift? But I sent the invitation anyway. Got a five dollar gift certificate for McDonalds. Guess he thinks we people don't eat steak. Can't afford it. No sense confusing our senses.

"I'll be with you no matter what you want to do," cried Belinda through her emerald eyes. She meant it, too. At least at the time. She saw me. Not my hair. Not an irresponsible lout trying to buck the system, but me, as me.

A week before our wedding, my birthday popped up in the draft lottery. We decided to wait to get married till I got back. I rushed down to the Army recruiting station and signed up so I could get into communications training.

"You can learn a trade," Daddy said. "It'll be good for you. Then when you get home you can get yourself a good job in the mill."

But I was just trying to stay out of the infantry. I had no quarrel with the North Vietnamese. I just wanted to stay out of the fight without going to Leavenworth for twenty years. So I signed up, but through some technicality that I still don't understand, I got stuck in the infantry anyway. Right there on the front lines in that bug infested jungle, fighting and killing just to stay alive.

I learned to hate the Cong. And I learned to hate Americans. They both tried to kill me every day. Damn them! Damn them all to hell! They're still trying to tell me how to live and die. My painting doesn't hurt anyone. I don't read the papers, and I'm not interested in the petty conditions of little factory towns or what those big management gods in Washington do next.

All I want is to be left alone. To paint. Blues and greens and yellows and purples. To live my life out without the worthless competitions of society. But if they don't leave me alone, I still know where I can get plenty of reds.

Is That Clock Right?

Some days I leave in what I think is plenty of time to get to class, only to find myself trying to sneak into a lecture-in-progress unnoticed. But of course, that's impossible. My shoes are wet from the snow and rain, and each step sounds like toilet plungers.

As I squish my way across the room, the instructor pauses for a few seconds, while everyone else just stares. I try to play it cool, find myself a seat, and pretend that I'm not late.

The instructor begins lecturing again, as I try to unzip my backpack. But it's a noisy affair that sounds as if it's coming through a bullhorn, so I carefully slow down the unzipping to a steady tick, tick, tick. I know without looking that other eyes are still staring, blinking with each annoying tick. I really want to just grab hold and yank it, one quick pain, like ripping adhesive tape off skin—hair and all. But that commotion would certainly be louder than this tick, tick, tick.

As always, something has to give. It's taking too long to get my pack open. I'm missing valuable notes, and I have to end those stares. So what do I do? I silently grasp the zipper with my left hand and steady the pack with my right. I listen to a few lines of lecture for the rhythm of words and phrases. Then we dance.

The instructor leads with the first word of a sentence, and I follow with the zipper, down past the verb. I stop. Waltz awhile, ballet awhile, but poised in position, I wait for that inevitable dip when I can push the zipper over the edge and down toward the floor. One side done, I switch hands and refrain. A few more steps and one more dip, my backpack is open.

Then I slowly gaze up toward the culprit of this predicament. The clock. I fantasize tying its lying little hands with its own ugly cord and drowning it face-first in that last shoe-deep puddle. But this clock is not the only one. It seems that every clock on campus is conspiring to make me late.

Some days, it takes me only a couple of minutes from one class to another, according to the arrival clock. Some days, fifteen. That's when I'm late. Then some days, I get there before I even leave.

Realizing that something has to be done, I search the campus for our resident clock watcher, Hans Turner. I find him up the hill in the gym, high atop a shaky ladder, a Windex sprayer hanging from the back pocket of his baggy overalls. He is scrubbing some invisible stain from the face of a clock, little paper towel pieces floating to the floor. I ask if he can spare a minute, and he says, "Sure!" And he wobbles down the ladder, the Windex sprayer swinging like a pendulum with each wobbly step.

I tell Hans my problem. He doesn't say anything as he stands there, rubbing his chin, staring up at the clock. I notice he isn't wearing a watch. A few seconds pass, and he looks back down at me, shaking his head.

"Well, I just can't understand it," he says. "I just checked all those clocks yesterday." That is all he says, and we both look up at the clock with the clean face.

My curiosity breaks the silence, and I ask him why he doesn't wear a watch.

"Don't like to take my work home," he says, shaking his head. Then he points to the clock. "I put in enough hours here with these guys. Ain't even got a clock at home."

I wonder aloud how he keeps up with the time.

"Well, I know when to quit by these clocks. I go to bed when the TV news goes off, and my old rooster wakes me up in the morning. My radio tells me what time it is then."

I try to imagine what makes some people tick.

"As far as these clocks go, I check 'em pretty often. There's a master clock in maintenance that my boss sets, and I make sure I get the right time off it before I go out. I even write it down."

He fumbles with some papers in his shirt pocket.

"I go around and set all those office clocks first, and then I come straight to the gym and set these. Then I go to the theater and the library, but then I do yard work and other stuff until about lunch time. Gives me a good appetite. After I eat, I go back to work inside, but the first thing I do is check that master clock again and write it down again. That's when I go through all the classrooms and set those clocks. I tell ya. They can't be that far off."

He chuckles and pats my shoulder.

"Maybe you just ought to leave a little earlier from now on."

I silently unwind as he picks up paper towel pieces. Then he shoulders the ladder and smiles.

"I'd like to stay and shoot the bull awhile, but I just ain't got the time today."

And he disappears through the doorway, the ladder trailing behind.

I stand there a few seconds, staring at the empty doorway. Then suddenly I realize that I'm late for class again. I look down at my watch, then up at the clock. I unfasten my watch, stuff it into my backpack, and head out the door and down the hill to my next class. But I don't run down. I take my time.

Gravity

"Do you think he'll show up?" Rick asked, tapping a half-eaten stick of red licorice against the wall calendar.

I just shrugged and headed with my groceries toward the checkout counter.

"Ain't missed one yet," said Curly, mouthing the lip of an empty Coke bottle and balancing his chair on its hind legs. He stared through the window of the little country store out at the spring rain. "Damn wacko." He siphoned one last drop of Coke and set the bottle down beside the chair.

"You shouldn't call him that." Rick shook his head as he limped back to the other old wooden chair beside the coal heater.

Curly jumped up, his chair thumping down hard on the wooden floor, the Coke bottle tumbling over and rolling with the distant thunder. "What the hell you talkin' 'bout? Look at your leg! Just look at it. You the one oughta be calling him a wacko. Damn Wacko!"

"Don't start this up again," said Rick, digging into the cellophane bag for another Twizzler.

"Don't start this up again," Curly mocked. "Far as I'm concerned, it ain't over yet." He pulled off his John Deere cap, ran his fingers through his thinning hair, and meandered over toward the Coke machine.

"We were trespassing, and it was dark, and it's been seven years now. For Christ's sake, leave it alone."

Curly put his cap back on and dropped his money into the slot. He stood staring at the buttons. His choices were Coke, Coke, Coke, and Coke. He pushed Coke. "Damn wacko shot a hole in your leg and a hole in my truck. It ain't over yet, and it won't be till he fixes my truck." He glanced out the window for the third time since I'd been there, popped the Coke lid open on the window sill, and ambled back toward his chair. "Gimme one o' them," he said, reaching forward for the licorice and sitting back at the same time, an impossible task.

Mr. Jordan looked up from bagging my notebook and bread and fresh-cut lunchmeats and just shook his head. "Yep, never fails when Johnny's coming home," he said. "Three dollars."

But that's the way it is back in these hills. They don't worry too much about sales tax, and Johnny's coming home is about the most exciting thing that happens here all year. This simple, serene existence is why I came here—and stayed.

I'd never lived in the country before, but with so many city interruptions, I couldn't concentrate on my sculpture. I'd ruined my last three attempts when door knocks and telephone rings pounded my chisel too hard, and weeks of work shattered into gravel. So one day, I just packed up my old Pontiac and drove off toward the Kentucky hills.

The first couple of nights, I pulled off into those little roads where tractors go to the fields, and I sat there way into the night just listening to owls and crickets and invisible creatures that came sniffing around my car in the dark. I kept my windows rolled up except for a small crack because it's still cold here in March. But I didn't mind. Every so often I'd run the motor for awhile to warm up.

I rented a little three room house from Old Man Jenkins, the next to the last house on a dead end road. It wasn't anything fancy, needed paint and the front porch was missing in spots, but it had a good fireplace and electricity, and if I hung a sheet over the kitchen doorway, the place was as warm and cozy as anywhere. Besides, for the rent I paid, I could live here a long time, a very long time.

Old Man Jenkins didn't mind being called just that. That's how he introduced himself to me through a snuff-stained smile, and he told me all about Johnny's place next door at the dead end, pointing toward the deserted shack with his walking cane. But it was more than just background. It was a warning—NO TRESPASSING.

Johnny's place was overgrown with dead rabbit tobacco stalks, withered Johnson grass and weeds, and maple saplings had sprung up head high all over. And what lawn I could see was thatched with sun-scorched crabgrass that choked the ground all the way down to the field.

The field. That's where the story grew. Directly between my place and Johnny's lay Johnny's field. Just about in its middle was a boulder as big as a VW Bug. The field had been turned under, but it was hard to tell when, and the plowing had bypassed the rock on all sides. But the rock was chipped, and pieces had been broken away at every angle that I could see.

Johnny had joined the Marines and gone off to boot camp just a week after his family bought the place and moved in. Evidently, Johnny and his father had argued about something, so Johnny just up and left. No one still seems to know exactly what the argument was about, and I've heard at least a dozen versions. But whatever the reason, Johnny's father and mother had avoided the subject.

Old Man Jenkins told me how pleasant but sort of frail Johnny's father was and how proud he was to finally have his own place. He had spent his life in the coal mines and just wanted to relax and farm and grow good things in the earth, not tunnel around in it like a mole anymore.

Johnny got word weeks later at boot camp about his father. He came home on a three day leave just in time to watch his father die of brown lung. They buried him on the first day of spring. Johnny's mother moved out of state somewhere to her sister's and left the house deserted. No one heard from Johnny till he came home three years later to an empty house and an overgrown field.

Old Man Jenkins said Johnny sat in that house for days, just staring out the window at that field. Then, on the first day of spring, Johnny went down to the co-op and rented an old beat-up tractor. He drove it back all the way, fourteen miles, in a wind that would take the paint off a barn. And he plowed that field. He plowed it all and finished in the late afternoon, that is, all but one spot.

Johnny threw a chain around that boulder and hooked it to the tractor, but no matter how hard he pulled, no matter how high he revved the engine and popped the clutch, that rock wouldn't budge.

The next day Johnny left, and no one heard from him for a whole year till he showed up again on the first day of spring, driving that same beat-up tractor down that dead end road.

Old Man Jenkins just shook his head and didn't say anything else as I handed him the rent money.

Mr. Jordan took the three dollars for my groceries, and I picked up my bag and walked to the door. I stopped and stared out at the rain, at Curly's old pickup and the bullet hole in his tailgate.

"Do you think he'll show up?" asked Rick. I turned, and he and Curly were both staring at me. Curly was mouthing another empty Coke bottle, and Rick rolled a fresh licorice stick back and forth between his thumb and finger, like a roll-your-own. I just shrugged again and bent down a little, looking up at the clouds.

Suddenly, the rain slacked up a bit, and I opened the door to head for my car. "See ya'll later," I said, but just then I heard the unmuffled chugs of some antique engine, and I looked up the road. Two dim headlights flickered and wobbled as the rain picked up again, and I stepped back inside and closed the door.

They heard it, too. And we all gathered at the window and watched in silence as an old beat-up tractor passed by, its bearded driver drenched in camouflage green, staring straight ahead as water ran off the bill of his cap. A heavy log chain lay wrapped around the tractor's rusty footrest, its end dangling over the side in midair, as the old tractor slowly disappeared down the road into the pouring rain.

Curly let out a heavy sigh and meandered off toward the Coke machine. "Damn wacko," he mumbled.

Rick limped over to the candy rack and picked up a fresh pack of licorice. Mr. Jordan headed back to the counter, and on his way, he picked up a fifty pound sack of flour and put it back down just two inches to the left, straining all the while. I glanced back out at the rain then walked over to Curly's empty chair by the heater. Rick was already sitting, tearing the licorice open with his teeth.

I set my bag on the floor beside the chair. "Gimme one o' them," I said as I leaned forward for the licorice and sat back at the same time, an impossible task.

Lightning

I'm standing on the patio one summer night when all of a sudden the sky lights up, and this big ball of fire flies over the house, big as a hot-air balloon, and my pony is going nuts out in her stall, kicking the walls and snorting something crazy. She's made all kinds of noise already, and that's why I'm out here in the first place.

"Go see what's wrong with her," my dad says from the den and rattles the newspaper. But I know what's wrong with her. It's what's wrong with me. But I can't speak, and my legs won't move. The fire flies over the cornfield and disappears behind the hill. It's landed. I know it's landed, and here I am stuck to the patio and can't even tell anybody. I swivel my body around on my stuck feet and see my dad standing in the doorway. He's looking out toward the hill.

I finally get some words out. "Did you see that?"

He just looks at me and nods and walks back into the den. But he's that way. Real religious and all. Probably thinks it's some bad omen or a sign from God or something. I just can't believe he walks away and leaves me here. I finally unstick my feet from the concrete and run out toward the stall. "Shut up, Kit!" But she's kicking and whinnying and not paying me any mind.

I stay far enough back so I can see the stall door and the spot at the hill where the fire disappeared. Maybe it'll take off again. I hope it don't. But Kit's kicking and snorting, so I walk on up to the stall. "It's all right girl."

Her black sides are jerking in the blue of the security light, and she's sweating something fierce. She sees me and calms down a little, and I grab a handful of sweet-feed and hold it out to her. But she won't take it. She just stands in the back of the stall, staring at me.

I stuff what'll fit of the sweet-feed into my mouth and drop the rest over the rail into the stall. She's stopped jerking so much, so I ease over to the side and look out at the cornfield. Nothing. No fire, no lights. Nothing. But it's landed. I know it's landed.

There's some shuffling inside the stall. I ease back over, and Kit walks up to me. I pat her on the head, she snorts, and I get her another handful of sweet-feed. Good stuff, that sweet-feed. We both stand there chewing for a few seconds, and I turn and ease back toward the house so I don't spook her. I keep looking over my shoulder back at the cornfield, but nothing. No sound. No explosions, no Air Force jets bombing. Nothing.

He won't let me go. I do everything but get down on my knees, but he won't let me go. He says there ain't nothing out there. Says it's too dark. But I tell him I saw it and that he said he saw it, too.

"Lightning," he says and picks up the Bible and starts reading while I'm just standing.

"But—"

"I told you. It's too dark."

I take one last look out the patio door and see that past the glow of the security light, it is dark. Black. I can't even see the cornfield. And quiet. Kit's not kicking anymore, and all I hear is a few crickets cricking back and forth across the yard. I just look at my dad, still reading his Bible, and head off toward my room.

I leave the light off, but I can't see toward the cornfield out my window. I always felt like my room faced the wrong way. Now I'm sure. I open the window to see if I can hear anything. Crickets, nothing but crickets. I turn on the light just long enough to find my radio and then sit there in the dark listening for any news about fire balls. There's baseball and softball and hail the size of golf balls somewhere in the next county, but nothing about fire balls.

I leave the radio on and the window open just in case and crawl into bed and lie there staring at the dark. It's landed. I know it's landed. And tomorrow, I'm going to saddle up Kit, and we're going to take off across that cornfield and over that hill and find it. And just in case anybody's in it, I'm going to take along some of that sweet-feed for 'em. Good stuff, that sweet-feed.

Leaving Alone

Frank sat on the barstool, holding a sweating beer, staring at the mute television, as the jukebox scratched out an old country song—"If I said you had a beautiful body...." Laughter from weekend drunks drowned out most of the words, while over-the-hill athletes wearing oversized headphones spat statistics from the silent screen. But Frank had been working on his own strategy.

For hours he had sat there thinking about Eleanor. Out of all the nights he'd seen her at the bar, she had never left with anyone. Frank couldn't understand it. To him, Eleanor was pretty—very pretty. She was somewhere in her mid-thirties, with long, wavy brown hair, always a pleasant smile, and he'd never seen her yell at any of the guys about anything. Some of them would sit with her for awhile, but sooner or later another girl would show up, and they'd make some lame excuse to end the conversation. The easiest one was to go to the bathroom and never come back. But Eleanor knew. She would just light up another cigarette and watch the crowd in silence through the mirrors behind the bar. And the bartender knew. He wouldn't embarrass her, though. He would just politely take away the drinks they left behind and pretend nothing happened.

Frank knew that these things hurt Eleanor, and he felt many times like telling those guys what jerks they were. But he never did. He just sat there on his regular stool and watched the crowd through the mirrors. He mostly watched Eleanor, that is, when she wasn't looking his way. He thought she had caught him staring a couple of times, but she never said anything. He would look away quickly and not look back for a long time, just in case.

But tonight he had sat there long enough to get up his courage. He realized that he had always been shy, too shy to just walk up and say hello, but tonight he had to try something. It was her presence and nothing else that drew him back to this place every weekend—her hair, her smile, her loneliness. If it was anything like his own, he knew how empty life could be and didn't want her to have to be so alone.

Frank glanced down into the mirrors again, and there was Eleanor at the other end of the bar. He hadn't seen her come in. It must have been during his daydreaming. He wasn't going to take any chances tonight, though, so he didn't stare at her through the mirrors and looked back up at the TV. He thought about his strategy again. He just knew it was going to work.

First, he would send over a drink, anonymously. Then he would keep an eye on that drink through the mirrors. This drink out of nowhere would surely get her curiosity up. When that drink was almost gone, he'd send her another, but this time he'd have the bartender tell her who sent it. That would be the deciding factor. Would she just smile with a friendly toast? Or would she invite him down to sit with her? Whatever she did, Frank had thought about it long and hard over several drinks of his own, and he was going to walk up and say hello no matter what.

He took another drink of his beer and set it down and twisted it around on the coaster, trying to line up the bottom of the bottle with the coaster logo of a beer he'd never even heard of. But he knew he was just wasting time. He leaned back on the stool and took a deep breath. A flash of light drew his gaze to the mirrors, and Eleanor was lighting up a cigarette. He looked away quickly, but he knew it was now or never. Brandy Old-Fashioneds. That's what she drank. Brandy Old Fashioneds, never anything else.

He reached into his pocket and pulled out his wallet, but then he just sat there as the weekend drunks laughed, loud and unnatural, maybe at some stale joke they'd all heard before. Frank closed the wallet, slipped it back into his pocket, and sat staring at his beer again. He didn't look up into the mirrors at Eleanor, but he thought about her. He wanted her. He wanted to take her home, forever. And as the sweat rolled down the bottle onto the soggy coaster, he wondered if those drunks had really been laughing at the joke, or at him, when he had reached into his pocket and pulled out his empty wallet.

Jump

Bo stood three jumpers back from the ledge. He squinted at the May sunlight slicing through the cedars, their heady scent lying stagnant around the muddy trail. Laughter and splashing rose from the river below, but the people and the water were hidden from where he stood.

Little River Canyon had attracted its usual Sunday afternoon crowd for booze, dope, swimming, and bush rattling. And earlier that day before crossing the bridge, Bo had descended the well-worn path on the other side of the river and walked along the bank, just staring up at this ledge. He didn't know anyone at the river that day, and he had come alone. On purpose.

This ledge didn't seem so high from down there. Sixty feet at the most. And guys were jumping off one after the other. City boys with store-bought tans and corrugated bellies and farm boys with sickly white chests and t-shirt lines. Even girls, sometimes. One had lost her top when she jumped, and Bo stood gawking until she saw him, looked down and screamed, and grabbed the nearest towel.

That had reminded him of Cindy. When she gave oral reports in class, her own chest heaved with each breath, and Bo found himself squirming in his seat, longing to bury his face in her sweater.

And next Saturday was the prom.

Bo had stood in front of the "Boys" bathroom mirror trying to control his nervous trembling. "No, no," he mumbled, pressing his fists against his quivering stomach and breathing heavily to calm himself. Just thinking about asking Cindy to the prom seemed so ridiculous! She wouldn't be caught dead with a geek like him.

Finally, he relaxed and with one last glance in the mirror he thought, *One small step for man—*

Bo caught up with Cindy at her locker, and after a couple of false starts, he took the plunge and blurted it out so loud that others stopped and stared. But she turned from her locker and gave him that heavenly smile that he dreamed about nights before falling asleep, and with her perfect lips and heaving chest she said, "Yes, Yes!"

The front jumper disappeared over the ledge with "Geronimo!" and soon a deep ker-plush echoed up the canyon walls. Bo took two steps forward as the line moved, then looked around behind him. No one. The jumpers must all be mellowing out on the boulders below. The only one left in front of him turned and offered Bo a joint, but Bo just smiled and shook his head.

The jumper mumbled something about not wanting to waste it as he leaned over and squeezed water from his hair to douse the joint. He flicked off the wet ashes, popped the joint into his mouth, chewed and swallowed.

Something jerked in Bo's stomach at the sight of this, and the taste of morning eggs passed over his tongue. Grimacing as nausea flowed throughout his body, he looked away into the cedars. They were fuller and taller than the ones down by the river. He remembered those well.

It was only a year ago when he lay at their scraggly, protruding roots, staring up into their sun-starved limbs. He had been on the other side of the river where another ledge provided a shallower jump for the less brave. Or less stupid.

He had jumped at least ten times that day and was about to go again when his foot slipped. Instead of jumping out toward the water, he dropped straight down, crashing through those outcropping cedars onto the rocks below. A pain shot up his left leg, and he screamed before he caught himself, fighting back tears as a crowd gathered at the edge and stared down at him.

After six weeks on crutches, he went back to the canyon. But every time he looked over that ledge, dizziness overwhelmed him, and his body trembled out of control. He finally gave up and left the canyon to the sure-footed or stoned.

All year, it had bothered him. It lay there at the bottom of his mind like he had lain on those rocks. The pain. The embarrassment.

And now he was about to graduate, but deep inside he knew that he wasn't ready. He knew that there was one final test he had to take and pass before he could walk across that stage and accept that scroll that says he is an adult, that he can step out into the world with knowledge, and without fear.

A "Yee-hi!" brought Bo back to the ledge. He knew it was time. There was no one in front of him anymore. And there was no one behind him to egg him on. It was his choice, alone. He didn't walk to the edge. He didn't move. He just stood staring at the empty space past the ledge where his world would either end or begin.

He thought of walking back across the bridge to the lower ledge, but he knew that, even if he could find the nerve, that smaller jump was just not enough. He looked down at his tennis shoes, at the mud and cedar needles sticking to them, and wondered if the river rocks would pierce right through even if he did make it. He listened to the laughter and splashing somewhere below.

Easing forward, he saw the river. Little River, snaking through the trees from the north, down into the gorge, then slithering back into the trees to the south. Little River Canyon, the deepest gorge east of the Mississippi.

What the hell am I doing up here?

Bo shook his head and inched closer to the edge. He began to tremble. Grabbing his stomach with both hands, he gritted his teeth and mumbled. *NO, NO.* Stopping a foot from the edge, he watched the people below him. No one was paying him any mind. That was good. He breathed heavily, and the trembling subsided a little. That was good, too. He realized he was not dizzy, even as he watched a runaway tractor tube float past the spot he'd have to hit, a large red patch on the tube's side slowly circling, circling. And there were trees and rocks below. He'd have to jump even farther than he did from the little ledge. Yes, little. He had never jumped from this high ledge, and from up here, the river looked at least a hundred feet down. Small and shallow, like a trout stream or rain-filled ditch. The underwater boulders beckoned around the clear pool where he'd have to land. Or else.

He thought about those who had actually died from this jump. Drunk, doped up, or crazy enough to jump when the water was muddy. They

49

had all missed that tiny underwater pool.

Bo thought about Cindy. He would never know what it would be like to bury his face there. Would she go to the prom without him? Would they have a moment of silence at graduation? And would somebody else stand here someday, thinking about him who had died from this jump?

The trembling worsened, and he pressed his fists against it. *No, No.* He tried to convince himself, but the shaking wouldn't stop. He took a deep breath and eyed the pool. Stepping back three steps, he stopped and thought. About nothing. His mind was a total blank.

He stepped forward with his right foot followed by his left, now running, and when his right foot touched the edge he knew there was no turning back. The emptiness swallowed him as he stepped into space, and he realized that he had forgotten to yell. Something. Anything! No one would notice, and no one would know. No one but him.

The river grew and grew, and the water rushed up at him till his shoes smacked the surface. He sank into the hollow blurbs of rising bubbles till his feet crammed into the rocky riverbed, letting his knees give way to the impact. He looked up and rose slowly toward the sun, limp, weightless.

His head emerged into river splashes and casual laughter. Wiping his eyes, he kicked to stay afloat, then flowed into a lazy, dog paddle. Pulling himself up onto a smooth, vacant boulder, he rolled over and lay silent in the warm sunlight. He realized the trembling had stopped and laid his hands flat on his stomach. Yes, it had stopped.

Propping up on one elbow, he looked back at the river then up at that empty ledge. Smiling, he thought about Cindy and wondered what she would wear to the prom. *Yes, Yes!*

Something Somebody Cooked Up

We were driving south in the Gulf of Mexico, and water spread out forever on both sides. Yep, I said driving. A hundred years before, it was all water. The pickup's radio blasted as we sped down that skinny, two-lane road. I had dibs on the window, and between the radio and gusts of wind, I couldn't hear half the conversation. That was okay, though. So far, the evening was perfect.

The four of us, Red, Rick, Brian, and I, had decided to skip town that Sunday, our only day off from performing music at the Holiday Inn. Mobile, Alabama, wasn't so crowded with tourists that time of year, and the locals really liked our band, but an extended contract, that time six weeks, always made us antsy.

So, after a few coin tosses, we decided to head off to Dauphin Island to check out its local cuisine. According to Red's old beat-up map—it went perfectly with his beat-up truck and beat-up guitar—Dauphin Island was about thirty miles south of us—only three miles wide. One thing was for sure. We wouldn't get lost. That was the only road.

We argued for awhile, that is I put in my two cents worth when I could hear, about whether an island was still an island if there was a land-filled causeway to it. A pothole sloshed Red's Budweiser onto his beard, but he never left the argument. Nodding his windblown curls, wiping his beard with one hand, and pointing skyward with the beer, he left the driving to divine spirits. He said God made islands, and they would always be islands.

Of course, Rick, a short, loud-mouthed New Yorker and devout atheist, jumped in with both feet, pointing at the map as if it were his college degree. He did that sometimes, arguing points with examples we never understood, his stocky frame trembling when he "knew" he was right. Now and then we'd let him win an argument anyway because good keyboard players were hard to find on the road.

Brian, the bass player, just sat sipping his own Bud, grinning all the while, but never saying much. He was like that—quiet, reserved—but he was the best bass player I'd performed with in years. He was just one of those towering, silent types that nobody messed with, and he didn't mess with them.

Finally, we all agreed that bridges leave islands intact, but we didn't settle anything about causeways. The sign settled it—Dauphin Island. We slowed down to about forty-five, even though the limit was twenty-five, but that was slow enough, Red said. He was hungry. We all were.

Glancing over at Red then back at the road, I thought about what he said about God and realized that he reminded me of a red-headed preacher who used to spit fire and brimstone at me when I was a kid. My family never missed a service. Thursday night, Saturday night—that supposedly kept the church members holy—and twice on Sunday. And that one road in front of the truck was like that one road to heaven the preacher spat about. The only road. If you were not on it, you were lost.

The Bible was so thick why did they always rehash the same things over and over again? Sure, I've always wanted to believe, and after so many years of Sunday practice, I felt as if I should be on my way to church somewhere right then. But so many things didn't make any sense. How could so many people believe in something that had no proof whatsoever? Why the wars? The starvation? Why did He let my birth mother die and my natural father disappear before I even knew them? Why wouldn't He just let me believe in Him without question? And why the hell was I thinking about that in the first place?

As I sighed heavily, the humid odor of salt water and dead fish brought me out of my trance, and I raised the sweating beer can to my forehead and said, "Kinda hot, ain't it?"

I looked around and Red and Rick and Brian were looking back at me with blank stares. Then I realized I had interrupted some conversation about a girl Rick had tried to put the make on the night before.

"What was her name again?" I asked and took a couple of swallows of beer to break the ice. It must have worked since they started talking about that girl again and didn't say anything about my mental lapse.

On down the road we passed a couple of places, run down dives with dirty windows and half-lit Pabst signs, but those joints didn't look too appetizing. A little farther on, I spotted another sign. It had a scaled-down version of an old wooden ship with three sail-less masts. The ship was grounded in a sand bar where "THE FINAL PORT" stuck out in wooden letters. Red must have spotted it, too, and turned into the parking lot, stopping that old pickup between a Caddy and a Beamer. No one argued about the restaurant.

The building wasn't as fancy as the sign, so we decided to risk it with our blue jeans. As we walked in, the room spread out before us. It was huge. Red said it looked like a converted bowling alley, and we agreed. The hostess, a young feisty brunette with a deep tan and pearly smile, led us through a smorgasbord of people. Everyone from farmers in overalls to male mannequins in tuxedos and ladies in sun dresses and what looked like evening gowns. We sat down at a table for twelve, but there was only us four. I didn't notice where she got them, but the hostess produced four thick books and gave one to each of us. The covers were worn black leather, and in the bottom right corner in gold letters, they read, "CAPTAIN'S LOG." The waitress smiled and pranced away, and for a few delicious seconds, we watched her and forgot about food.

The settings were fancy, water and wine glasses and coffee cups and enough silverware at each spot for all four of us. Soon, the waitress showed up again, and Red ordered a highball. I decided it was time I did some serious drinking, my day off and all, so I ordered a Southern Comfort on the rocks. Rick and Brian stuck to beer. Somebody had to drive back.

While we waited for our drinks, I noticed I already had a serious buzz. But that was okay. I just needed food. Not until then did I notice the aroma of unfamiliar dishes all around me. Some good, some bad, and some I wasn't sure if the culprits should be eaten or buried. Opening the CAPTAIN'S LOG, I found that the front and back covers were one-inch thick solid fakes made to look like pages. The real menu was

in the middle—only about six pages. I had heard of some of the dishes—
squab, cacciatore, vichyssoise, but I'd never eaten them. At least, I
didn't remember eating them. I sat wondering for a moment what baby
pigeon and chicken were doing on that menu. But I hadn't traveled to
the middle of the Gulf of Mexico to eat pigeon.

I found the seafood list, plain-language dishes, thank goodness, and
looked it over. Trout, sea bass, squid, octopus?—yuk! Then I saw it.
Seafood gumbo. Cajun food. Something about it made me want it. I'd
never eaten it. Never even seen it. But I wanted it. Closing the menu, I
announced that I was ready to order. Of course, the waitress was
nowhere in sight. It was evidently one of those places that serves you
in one big spurt, holding back your order like a submerged whale, then
suddenly emerging, spraying torrents of food on your table, giving no
time to duck.

We all passed on salads for another drink...and another...and another.
After submerging in that many drinks, you lose all track of time and
forget that you've been waiting forever. I sat hoping I wouldn't have to
go to the bathroom. I didn't think I could even walk.

Finally, the waitress headed for our table, carrying a huge tray piled
with food. It was the big spurt that I had expected. She set the tray on
a nearby stand and started her rush to give us the plates. First, Red
with his steak and shrimp, Rick with his perch, Brian with his roast
beef. Then the waitress slowed down a bit. She turned around from the
tray, holding a gigantic white bowl that was as big as a belly-up sea
turtle, and marched slowly toward me. She set the bowl in front of me,
and I stared into it, trying to focus as best as I could.

Everyone at the tables around us suddenly became very quiet. They
had seen the big bowl, too. As my vision cleared, the strong aromas of
fish and pepper and garlic and whatever else was in that bowl invaded
my nostrils, and my eyes began to gloss over again.

I stared into the bowl into what appeared to be black swamp water,
pieces of wood and weeds and garbage floating in it, and I didn't move.
Then suddenly, something rose up slowly from that black abyss and
broke the surface. I sat staring in the silence as two black eyeballs
emerged, staring back at me. A huge crawdad settled on the surface,

menacing and angry, looking as though it were about to attack. My eyelids were stretched to the limit. I looked up at the waitress who stood grinning, and Red burst into uncontrolled laughter that spread throughout the whole restaurant.

Rick and Brian joined in, and as I looked around, there were tears and smiles and knee slapping everywhere. That's when I lost it and burst out laughing myself. Red handed me a knife and said I'd better kill that thing before it got loose, and a second wave of laughter roared throughout the restaurant.

After a short while, everything was calm again, and I was on my way to being sober. It took me some time to take that first spoonful, but believe it or not, that gumbo was excellent. Those pieces of wood and weeds and garbage were the best things I had eaten in a long time. I dipped the spoon around the crawdad till there was no gumbo left, then I stuffed the crawdad into a doggy bag for a later bug-eyed snack.

When we headed back to Mobile, Brian got behind the wheel, and Rick and I shifted one spot to the left for Red. Down the road a bit, Brian reached over the seat and pulled out a warm six-pack, popped one open, and Red said that little island had pretty good eats. Rick said it was really a peninsula now, and the whole beer-waving, sky-pointing, frame-trembling argument started all over again. Brian just smiled and sipped on his warm Bud. The doggy bag crinkled in my lap, and I decided to take a peek. As I opened up the bag, Red mentioned God again right when those two little black pearls stared straight up at me.

Leprechaun Logic

For a week now, I've had him locked in the basement, and he's driving me crazy.

It all started during a thunderstorm. I was driving precariously through the rain and fog, my windshield wipers backstroking in an airborne sea, when I heard a thump. I was only driving about 15 and stopped fast.

Once out of the car, I looked back down the road. It was hard to see through the rain, but an old hound dog was staring at me as he stood beside the road. I wondered if he was hurt. He growled at me and barked, then trotted away. I figured I must have just stunned him.

But getting back into the car, I heard HIM. No, not the dog. HIM. I ran around the car toward the ditch, and there he lay, mud covered and soaked to the bone. Lying beside him was a small, overturned metal bowl, kind of like a little spittoon, with shimmering yellow coins spilling from it into the ditch. I thought my eyes were surely playing tricks on me when he groaned again and rubbed his forehead with his muddy little hand.

"Are you okay?" I asked and reached down to help him up.

He stumbled to his feet and glared up at me through glimmering blue eyes. In a thick Irish brogue, he yelled.

"Why don't ya look where you're going?" He snarled and kicked me in the shin.

"Hey! I didn't see you. I was just—"

"Yeah, yeah, I bet. And why don't ya feed your little beastie?" he snarled again, pointing toward the dog who was watching us from down the road. "So he won't go chasing people around."

"But he's not my—"

"I guess it's me gold you're after anyway. Is it?" He kicked the bowl and grabbed his toe. "Well, take it! It's yours. I'm tired of lugging the darned thing around every time it rains."

I stood staring at this two-foot high, redheaded elf, dressed in sneakers, jeans, and a flannel shirt, as he picked up a pointy green hat and tried to brush it clean.

He looked up at me and scowled. "Close your mouth, or you're gonna drown."

I looked at him in disbelief. "Are you really a—"

"Don't ask questions. Just take the gold and be off with ya." He hesitated, then added, "Here, I'll help ya pick it up." We scrambled through the ditch for every last coin. Just as I dropped the last one in, he grabbed the pot with both hands and took off running. Both steps, that is. He slipped in the mud, and down he went. This time the gold didn't spill, and I grabbed the pot out of his hands. With fake fear in his eyes, he glanced down the road.

"I thought I saw the beastie again."

"Yeah, right," I thought aloud as I headed for the car, carrying the gold. As I got in, I heard the pitter-patter of little feet running up to me. I left the door open to see what he wanted.

"Wait! Wait! You really don't want that gold, do ya? You'll just spend it, and it'll be all gone. But let me tell ya. I can give ya something even better than that gold."

I looked down at the little pot resting on my lap. "I thought you didn't want it."

He shuffled his tiny feet in a puddle of water. By that time the rain had become only a drizzle.

"I was just a wee bit mad," he said. "Ya see, it's been raining a lot lately, and every time there's gonna be a rainbow, I've got to lug that darned pot to where the rainbow's gonna end. I'm practically worn out."

I mulled over what he had said for a minute then asked, "How do you know which end of the rainbow to put the gold under?"

"Well, bless me ancestors that kissed the Blarney Stone. This one just might have a brain."

"Which end?" I asked again.

"Under the right end," he frowned. "Don't ya know which end is the right end? If I left it on the left end that would be the wrong end, so I leave it under the right end 'cause the right end is the right end. Don't ya know that's why ya got a right hand and a wrong hand?"

"But—"

"Questions, questions."

"But what if you're on the other side of the rainbow? Then the left end is the right end."

The little man patted his shamrock necklace and spoke up to the sky.

"Well, I thought he had a brain."

He held the necklace with one hand as he waved his arm through a big arc then pointed around the arc.

"Look here, Einstein. If you're on the other side of a rainbow, there ain't no rainbow. And it don't take a genius to figure that out."

I didn't like his tone, so I closed the door. Immediately, he started pounding away on it. I looked down again at the gold shimmering in the pot, then rolled down the window. He stopped pounding and backed away from the car so he could see me.

"Listen. Here's what I'll do," he said. "Ya gimme back me gold, and I'll grant ya a wish. Anything ya want."

This time he really looked sincere, and I knew if he gave up his gold, he'd lose all his powers, at least that's what my grandpa once told me. "Can I think awhile about what wish I want to make?"

He hesitated a moment then squinted one eye at me.

"Yeah, ya can do that. But by midnight on St. Patrick's Day, if ya ain't got a wish by then, the deal is off, and I get me gold back."

"It's a deal," I said, "but only if you let me lock you up until I make my wish."

"Lock me up? Why the devil would ya want to lock me up?"

"Because I know that 'con-man' came from the word 'Lepre-chaun-man.'"

His eyes narrowed as he stared at me, but soon he glanced down at a puddle in the road and sighed heavily. "It's a deal," he said, reluctantly.

Well, that's how it all began. He eats six times a day, and if I have to cook potatoes again, I'm gonna throw up. My liquor bill is turning into a second mortgage, just trying to keep him sedated. I don't know where he puts it all.

Oh, no. There he goes again, singing. If he sings "Danny Boy" one more time, I'm gonna strangle that little red faced runt.

I know it's mostly my fault, though. I can't make up my mind what to wish for. One wish, that's all I get—the most important decision of my life.

There goes that song! I wish he would—WHOAH!!!

I have to clear my mind. Let's see—the square root of seventeen is equal to the amount of pancakes it takes to sink a battleship in a hurricane or to the amount of feathers on an Amazonian chicken-lizard during mating season. . . .

There. That was a close one!

I almost lost my wish to something stupid. I've made a wish-list, and I have until midnight—St. Patrick's Day—one I'll never forget!

Wish me luck.

Ripples in Silence

I lay on my side in the hammock, staring from the deck of the houseboat out over Lake Prophet into the starlit sky. The gibbous moon, only half risen over the Appalachians, cast its soft light onto the rolling tips of distant pines. The water lay still, the mirror image, sharp and clear, broken only by the occasional jump of a hungry young bass leaping for the twinkling morsels above.

The hammock swung lazily as I shifted and eyed my three companions, Junker, Fisher, and Lamar. They each gazed quietly at the rising moon or the flickering dock lights two miles away, perhaps at a spot where love once nibbled, but reeling in too late, only an empty hook emerged. And behind us another mile, the opposite shore lay in darkness, where the moon would eventually sink slowly behind the foothills, long after we had slumbered.

For years now, one week in late autumn, we had gathered at the Big Copper Dam to fish and reminisce, where trophies waited just below the surface, and tales trickled down mountain streams into the lake, surrounded us as if everything had happened only yesterday. It was that time of year when evening chills settled on the water, and the summer boaters packed up their sails and headed home. And the nights echoed with an undisturbed silence, like deep sleep.

The Jenny Sue had always been good to us. She was an aging thirty-foot houseboat that we reserved every year, not much to look at alongside the new outriggers around the docks, but still as seaworthy as ever. Just sentimental old fools, I guess some called us, but stepping onto her deck, her pontoons resonating hollow splashes, made us all feel young again, and each voyage was a trip back in time.

A slight scrape of fiberglass against metal brought my gaze to Junker. He now sat half snoozing in a lawn chair, his feet propped up on Jenny

Sue's railing, a fishing pole bobbing up and down between them. Some sly trophy had just stolen his bait, and after mumbling under breath, Junker squirmed in his chair and dozed off again without even checking his line.

Fisher puffed on that same old black pipe he brought every year. He claimed it was his fishing pipe ever since he pulled in that marlin down in the Keys. Supposedly, he had fought that fish for two hours, chewing on that pipe the whole time. Since then, he never went fishing without it. Claimed it was good luck.

Lamar stood silent back by the sleeping engine, leaning upon the railing, staring at the distant shore. He wasn't much of a fisherman, but he had traveled the Tennessee and Tombigbee Rivers for many years after World War I as a liaison for the Tennessee Valley Authority. Dam projects were springing up all over the South during that time, and Lamar had been one of those hired to ease the tensions between disgruntled landowners and the TVA.

It was Lamar who had chosen Lake Prophet as our first gathering place, and he requested that we return here each year. None of us ever argued since we all appreciated this quiet spot in the Tennessee wilderness, and I guess we all had our own reasons for returning. But the real reasons we had always kept to ourselves.

Lamar reached into his shirt pocket and pulled out a plug of Days Work chewing tobacco. He cut a small chunk with his Barlow and examined the piece in the moonlight. Evidently satisfied with its size, he stuffed the chunk into his mouth, opened wide, and bore down with the first chew. That first was always difficult because of his false teeth. But soon, the tobacco would soften, and his Days Work would become painless.

He spit over the rail, and the minute splash sent glistening, silent ripples into the night. Looking up again at the moon and stars and wiping his mouth with the back of his hand, he sighed heavily, then turned and ambled toward the bow. "I remember a night just like this," he said. "November, and the stars were so close Fisher could have lit his pipe on one."

"Uh, oh," said Fisher, his deep voice resonating across the water.

"Here he goes again."

He was right. Every night, Lamar had a different story to tell. His past life on these southern waters must have been a continuing adventure, but we figured that many of his stories were not completely true. Some had no moral resolutions to speak of and more often than not, no endings at all. But we also knew that aging turns belief into truth in one's own mind, and in Lamar's, every event was exactly how it happened.

Sometimes, Lamar's stories would float on for an hour or so, and just when the climax seemed to be around the bend, he would drop anchor and say that he didn't know how things turned out because he was called away on another assignment. But we really didn't mind. That's how life is. There were so many unfinished stories in our own lives. Maybe that's why we journeyed there each year—to search the waters, the mountains, and the skies for possible endings. Endings that would make our pasts easier to live with.

Junker had woken up and was mumbling to himself again as he rummaged through his tackle box, planning revenge on the bait thief that had disturbed him earlier. Lamar pointed an empty chair northeast toward the darkness at the head of the lake where the submerged river once meandered down its natural course. He spit over the rail again, sat down with a grunt, and continued his story.

Yes, it was a night just like this. I'll never forget it. This lake wasn't even here yet, and the Big Copper River ran right under where we're sitting. I'd been working on the Tombigbee over in Mississippi when I got a telegram to come here to Red Bluff. Said it was urgent.

Yeah, Red Bluff was a nice little town. Sat right above the dam, but it's under about a hundred and sixty feet of water now. Of course, they bulldozed it all first. They'd planned on putting locks here and didn't want somebody's roof jabbing through somebody's hull. But even after they bulldozed it, they decided locks would be too expensive. That's why all that's here is the power plant.

I left Mississippi and got here as soon as I could. Leroy Banks—I'd worked with him before—met me at the bus station. He had just arrived the day before, been working on some project on the Ohio up around

Marietta. Some barge wreck or something. Anyway, it was getting dark, and Leroy filled me in on the way across town to the docks, driving way too fast for the lights of that old Model-T. I don't know how we ever made it without crashing.

"It's Wilson," he said. "They sent him up river two months ago to settle things with the hold-outs. It seems he was doing fine for awhile. He sent reports back twice a week until two weeks ago. No one has heard from him since. They're going to close those gates at noon exactly three weeks from today. Lamar, you've got to go find him and get those people to understand that it's going through. The company wants me to stay here and make sure the word gets passed on."

I had heard of Wilson, but I'd never met him. Stories floated around the company about his work up and down rivers like the Nile and the Colorado. It seemed that he was always transporting some big wheel to somewhere to inspect some thing or another. They even said he spent six months on the Amazon, but no one seemed to know exactly what he was doing there. Company secret, I guess.

I'd always wanted to meet him, to be like him. Of course, battling treacherous waters and blood thirsty savages is very appealing till you have to do the fighting yourself. But there was more. There was a sort of mysticism about him—like the fog that comes from out of nowhere on the Mississippi, sneaks around the bend and swallows you, blurs your senses and fills you with doubts, then spits you back out a lesser man. Something unchangeable, untouchable, immortal to river men. I know it sounds vain, but I guess I just wanted to be remembered, to cut some permanent valley into this puny existence, a valley too mysterious and too deep, with zigzags all along its course, one that could never be flooded and forgotten. But I knew I could never be Wilson. He was already like the great white hunter along the rivers, and I was only an obscure missionary, hired to give out trinkets to the natives, to talk pretty to them, and tell them about a so-called better life waiting downstream. Of course, my pretty talk didn't always work, and that's when the politicians and the law stepped in. I wondered why the authorities hadn't stepped in here.

"What about the law?" I asked Leroy.

"They're not exactly helpful. If we have to depend on them to serve evictions, we're going to have some drownings on our hands. These people don't believe the water's coming, but nothing's going to stop it now. It's too far gone."

We passed by two parked bulldozers on the way, and Leroy informed me that the main demolition in the town was to start one week before the gates closed. That process never took long, though, especially with such a small town. They never cleaned up all of it, just what wouldn't burn but still might float and clog up the dam. They would bring the rest of the bulldozers from the dam site, and Red Bluff would be flattened in a matter of days.

As we approached the docks, I could see the dam in the distance. Its massive concrete wall rose at least two hundred feet above the rebellious waters of the Big Copper, but the river now flowed almost tame through three huge flood gates. The moon was fat that night, too, and the dam wall glowed sickly white, like some gigantic tombstone.

Leroy pulled up to the docks to a small steamer, not much bigger than the Jenny Sue. Her stack was already spitting smoke and ashes, and glowing lanterns hung at each end of her tiny deck. A young man, somewhere in his early twenties, stood by her railing.

"That's Chuck," said Leroy. "He knows this river up and down."

"Where's the captain?" I asked.

"You're the captain."

"Now wait a minute," I protested. "I haven't actually run a boat in years."

"Don't worry about it," laughed Leroy. "It's just like riding a bicycle. Besides, Chuck knows everything about her, and he'd get his license if he ever learned how to read."

"You mean he doesn't have a—" I stopped myself. I knew it was too late to argue. Besides, the company knew I always kept my license current. Leroy just smiled and nudged me onto the deck.

"Is there anyone else on board?" I asked.

At that moment, a big, muscular man stepped out from behind the wheelhouse. "This is Paul," Leroy said. "He'll keep your fire going. You shouldn't have any trouble. Chuck said it's only about seventeen miles upriver to where Wilson is, but there's not even one road that cuts through these mountains. This river is it."

I thought it over and decided quickly that there was indeed no use arguing. Those people had to be evacuated.

Leroy stood on the dock and watched as we headed out into the night. Chuck said we'd only be able to make about six miles that night because the river got too narrow and too shallow in spots to navigate in the dark. That was fine with me. And since he said our top speed was only about three knots against the current here, and even slower upriver, I already knew that it would take over two hours to reach that first stop anyway.

The minutes crawled along, with me at the wheel and Chuck on the bow watching for snags in the moonlit water. Paul hadn't said a word the whole time I was onboard, but he kept the steam up, and that was all I was worried about. If that little engine died, the Big Copper could grab us and sink us in no time at all.

After a seemingly endless time of chugging along, Chuck walked back toward the wheelhouse. "We'll have to stop her here," he said.

I pushed the lever to all-stop, and Chuck threw out the anchors, angled out from the bow, one on each side to keep us steady midstream. In the moonlight, I could see the river narrowing ahead, disappearing around a dark bend into the forest.

"Are you sure we won't bottom out?" I asked Chuck.

"I'm sure. I've been up here lots of times on this boat. We scraped her a few times, but we always made it."

Paul was unrolling his sleeping bag next to the wood pile, as Chuck opened a side door on the wheelhouse.

"You've got a cot here," Chuck said. "It fits right in front of the wheel if you squeeze it in."

"That's fine," I told him. "Where do you sleep?"

"I take my bag up top. I like to sleep under the stars if it ain't raining. I got used to it when my daddy used to take me hunting."

With that he scampered up the side of the wheelhouse, and I heard a few footsteps and the rustling of a sleeping bag above. I unfolded my cot and slipped into the bag the company sent for me. I wondered where it had been kept before this trip because it smelled strong of mildew. But after awhile, the night being so peaceful, I fell asleep anyway in spite of the repugnant odor.

The following morning, I was awakened by Paul shoving wood into the burner, and I raised up and noticed that Chuck was fishing off the bow. He heard me stir and started reeling in the line. I folded the cot, replaced it in the side door, and walked back to the engine. Paul was opening a can of coffee. A burn-stained coffee pot sat on top of the burner alongside a cast iron skillet. To my surprise, Paul had produced eggs and sausages from somewhere.

"Are you the cook, too?" I asked.

"Guess so." He grinned, and from that moment on I saw him in a different light. I hadn't known how to take him at first since he was so quiet, but now he seemed as gentle as a pet bear, and I felt good knowing he was onboard.

After breakfast we weighed anchors and headed upstream again. The day brightened as we chugged along, but because of the foothills, it would be awhile before the sun beamed over the treetops. Four hours passed uneventfully, but the river narrowed more and more till its banks closed in to about fifty feet on each side of us. The water flowed more swiftly now, and it was all our little steamer could do to make two knots against the current. Chuck assured me that it would get no worse as far as we would go.

Suddenly, shots rang out and the wheelhouse window burst into fragments. I ducked below the tiny wall as lead whacked against both sides of the steamer, and the boat swerved to the right with an unattended wheel. I reached up and hit all-stop, and we floated backwards toward the left bank and ground to a halt in the shallows. At least we weren't drifting. Finally, I got up the nerve to peek out the door. Chuck lay flat on deck, smiling curiously at me. There was a lull in the firing, and I bellied out on deck a little and saw Paul squatting beside the burner.

"Don't worry," said Chuck still smiling. "If they wanted to hit us they would've. These mountain men can shoot the eye out of a rabbit at a hundred yards. They're just trying to scare us off. They ain't too happy about giving up this land."

Paul crawled over to me and shoved a Tommy gun into my hands.

"Where the hell did you get that?" I asked.

"They said there might be trouble."

With that, he opened fire into the forest, and a rapid spray of bullets struck the trees alongside the river.

"Wait!" I yelled.

But he was already scurrying around the wheelhouse, and he fired into the woods on the opposite side. The shots from the forest ceased, and I could hear diminishing scuffling as the invisible shooters hurried off in retreat. We waited in silence till the rustling of bushes and leaves and stones disappeared.

I crawled over to Paul and attempted to jerk the gun from his hands before he even knew I was there. The gun wouldn't budge.

"Give me that gun," I demanded.

Paul looked at me for a moment, then handed me the weapon. He looked down at the woodpile and explained, "I was just doin' what they told me."

"What who told you?"

"Leroy."

I couldn't believe it—Leroy telling Paul to shoot people?

"Leroy said the big wheels said to scare 'em off if they was any trouble."

I felt relieved then that he was not supposed to shoot anyone. "If you were just supposed to scare them, why were you shooting right at them?"

"Ain't never shot no gun much. They just showed me once."

I saw the sincerity in his face and felt ashamed that I had prejudged him. I handed both guns to him. "Put them away, and don't get them out again unless I say so."

Paul nodded and took the guns back by the engine where he laid them in a small crate. I looked back at Chuck. He smiled and shrugged. After a moment, I shook my head and smiled back.

"You don't think they'll hurt us?"

"Naw," Chuck said. "They think we're just like revenuers. A few shots and off go most city fellers high tailin' back to town. Don't know

67

what they're gonna think about them Tommy guns, though. It might really get 'em riled up."

It wasn't long before we had the boat free again. Chuck had swum over to the other bank with a come-along and hooked it around a tree. With him cranking, Paul pushing waist deep in the river, and my steering, we finally dislodged the boat.

We travelled on upriver without incident and at dusk dropped anchor for the night next to a small clearing. We split the night watch into three-hour shifts, and I chose the three-o'clock. It seemed like only minutes after I climbed into my bag that Chuck was tapping my arm, whispering it was my turn. I was just beginning to roll up my bag when Chuck's footsteps shuffled above.

Out on deck, I stood against the railing, finally waking up completely in the chill of the river breeze. On shore, a bobcat with her kitten emerged from the bushes into the moonlit clearing, but seeing the boat, she stopped dead still. The kitten romped around her and took no notice, but the mother soon abandoned her thoughts of drinking and hurried off into the bushes, the kitten bounding behind her.

Such a sight always bothered me along the rivers of dam projects. Who warned the animals when it was time to leave, time to run for their lives? I'd seen hundreds of them washed up on shore, days after the gates close. Deer, and horses, pigs, even cows and dogs. And it always happens the same. As the water rises, they seek higher ground, but sometimes the high spots they think are safe turn into island traps. The water rises higher and higher, and the little islands shrink, forcing the animals closer and closer together. And in scared frenzies, some fall into the water and drown, while others stand shaking, not understanding the death that closes in. "You've got to get those people out," the company always said. But they never said anything about the animals. They didn't care about destroying nature, and deep inside, I always knew they didn't give a damn about the people either. They just hired guys like me to make them look good.

Somewhere deep in the forest, a bobcat wailed—maybe the same one. Was it anger? I couldn't blame it. Or was it a cry for help, for directions, some natural instinct, warning of the danger to come? *Such a waste*, I thought, just as the cat cried out again into the night and was answered by another, far downstream. *Such a waste.*

The next day, we rounded a bend about noon, and a little town, if you could call it that, emerged from nowhere along the banks of the river. There were no roads, but dirt trails threaded between several shacks of tin and weathered planks where ragged men led dusty mules loaded with pelts and boxes and dirty burlap bags. The hollowness of their faces matched the dull stares of the women and children who eyed us without expression.

"That's Kinleyville," said Chuck. "Don't worry. You ain't got nothing to be afraid of. They know me."

I chose to remain silent as I guided the little steamer up to the run-down dock. Chuck and Paul secured the lines as I pushed her to all-stop. I stepped slowly out on deck and for a moment gazed up and down the sloping river bank. Ten or fifteen small boats of all shapes and conditions of decay were being loaded by somber men and wrinkled women. They began to stare at me as if I were the Devil himself. A short man with a scraggly, gray beard and mud splattered cheeks walked over slowly from a nearby family who was loading their tiny raft. Faded pictures in homemade frames, bundles of flour sack dresses and faded overalls, stove scarred pots and pans, and a makeshift coop with chickens cackling above the silence.

"I told them it was all over," he said to me. "And I told them yesterday they could go ahead and try to scare you off, but it wouldn't do any good. I figured they'd send you, Lamar."

I finally realized that I was listening to the legend himself, Frank Wilson. It's funny, but I had always pictured him to be younger, taller, muscles like Errol Flynn. But there he was, just an ordinary little man, as dirty and forlorn as the people he had come upriver to lure from their homes to the promised land. I didn't know what to say, but somehow I spoke. "You know me?"

"You'd be surprised how fast word travels through these woods. It's better than the mail if you ask me."

"But why haven't you sent word to Leroy?"

"I guess I just didn't have anything to say." He looked around at the destitute faces that gathered around us. The people were so quiet it was unsettling. Most of the men wore pistols or carried rifles, and I knew that if anything broke out, Tommy guns or not, we were way outnumbered. It appeared they all looked at Wilson with the same hate they had for me. Wilson turned to me once again.

"I've spent all morning explaining it to them again. I did before, over and over, but this time I told them if you were coming it meant that it was really all over." He glanced toward the row of tiny boats lined along the bank. "Most of them are packing up now. They don't have much, and it won't take them long."

"What do you mean most of them? We've got to get every—"

"It won't do any good. They said they're going to stay. And believe me. They're going to stay."

I stood silent and glanced around at the pitiful town.

"Some of the men will bring the stock out by trail in a couple of days. I told them the company would buy anything they wanted to sell. They already know they'll get some money for their land." He turned around for the last time and gazed upon the people of Kinleyville. Then he stepped onto the deck. "That's all I can do. Let's get out of here."

I looked around for his luggage. "Where's your—"

"Don't have anything and don't want anything." He walked to the opposite side of the boat and stared downriver where his gaze remained as we left the dock. The little steamer chugged along faster as if hastening our retreat, and Chuck had to remind me several times that I'd better slow her down.

That night, as we lay at anchor, I approached Wilson who stood staring out toward the rolling skyline. He spoke softly as his words steamed into the brisk November air. "I can't do it anymore," he said. "This is the last time." He turned without looking at me and headed for the cot Chuck had prepared for him. "It's just not right," he mumbled as he climbed into his sleeping bag. "Just not right."

Chuck and Paul had already been sleeping for awhile, so I decided to stay up, even though we probably didn't need a watch that night. I leaned over the rail, watching leaves float downstream, and listened to the sounds of the forest. Somewhere, a whippoorwill whistled into the night, and sleepless squirrels argued over misplaced acorns. A doe and her fawn, evidently born late that year, walked quietly down to the water's edge. And while the mother drank from the river, the fawn suckled, and the river breeze passed over me like ripples in silence, and I felt the haunting cold of a living tomb.

The next morning, Chuck woke me at daybreak. "Mr. Wilson's gone."

It was true. There was no sign of him anywhere, but on his cot lay an old Barlow knife and a half-plug of chewing tobacco. We searched the woods for Wilson, yelling for him and looking for signs of a trail, but even if he had heard us, he never did answer. Finally, we abandoned the search. I knew somehow that he didn't want to be found. All I could do was return to Red Bluff and file a report while the office was still standing.

Two weeks later, they closed the flood gates, and the Big Copper began rising, inch by inch, day by day. But I never got to see Lake Prophet take shape. As usual, I was called off on another assignment, this time to Kentucky, to start the whole process all over again.

Junker raised up in his chair. "I never heard all this story before. Besides, I thought you said you quit after you met that guy Wilson."

"I did quit. I got to that little town in Kentucky, and I could swear I saw the same faces I'd seen in Kinleyville. I stayed a couple of nights, but that was all I could stand. I turned in my resignation and told them I was through with the whole business. They wanted to know what was wrong, but I never told them. I left them to figure it out for themselves."

With that, Lamar spit over the railing and small ripples spread out on the water, glistening through the thick, November air. Junker sighed heavily, mumbled something about TVA, and tightened the tension on his reel. And Fisher, he snored quietly, that old black pipe hanging loosely between his lips ever since he had dozed.

I turned over in the hammock and lay there feeling insignificant between the vast waters and sky. Then an unfamiliar guilt began to rise all around me, higher and higher, as I thought about Lamar's story. But why should I feel guilty? I had nothing to do with any of it. But no matter how I tried to ignore the guilt, it continued to rise, even as the night engulfed me. And just as I began to doze, small bubbles sounding like tiny slurpings emerged from deep within the lake, and somewhere in the distant mountains, a bobcat cried.